From Riches to Bitches

Pick of the Litter

From Riches to Bitches

Pick of the Litter

Louise F. Shattuck

Edited by Brenda E. Abbott

Photographs and Drawings by the Author

Published by Hoflin Publishing, Inc.

From Riches to Bitches

This book is dedicated to the loves of my life.

Copyright 1996 by Louise F. Shattuck

ISBN 0-86667-053-X

All rights reserved. No part of this book may be used or reproduced in any manner whatsoever without written permission from the publisher, except in the case of brief excerpts quoted in reviews.

Hoflin Publishing, Inc.
4401 Zephyr St.
Wheat Ridge, Colorado 80033 U.S.A.
303/934-5656
email donh@hoflin.com

10 9 8 7 6 5 4 3 2 1
Printed in U.S.A.

Contents

The Author		7
Forewords		11
I.	The Sub-Culture	13
II.	Days of Our Lives	26
III.	The Breeding Game	48
IV.	Dog Shows	59
V.	Ties that Bind	79

Self portrait of the author

The Author
by Brenda E. Abbott

Louise F. Shattuck's writings and cartoons about her life with dogs are delightful. The recipe for this collector's edition anthology was to take the best of her two previous books, *From Riches to Bitches* and *In Stitches Over Bitches*, add plenty of new material, blend in lots of rib-tickling cartoons, and stir briskly! These pages are full of poignant observations and funny experiences that are easily recognized by anyone who breeds, shows, or simply shares a life with dogs. Her funny, honest, sometimes droll, retelling of the Carry-On Cockers' canine antics are guaranteed to touch a few chords in all of us, bringing lots of chuckles and maybe even a tear or a two.

A native Bostonian, Louise Shattuck demonstrated early a natural talent for art as well as a love of animals. In time, these two strong suits together developed her into one of America's foremost dog artists. She graduated with a BFA from the Massachusetts College of Art and developed a successful career as a teacher of sculpture and ceramics. For many years she taught in private schools and also conducted evening art classes in and around Boston. The scope of Louise's artistic talent and her popularity as a teacher further enhanced her reputation and the esteem for her work. Free-lance commissions were frequent, and she has sculpted numerous pieces for the windows and interiors of some of New England's most fashionable retail stores. She once sculpted a group of life-size animals used in a huge nativity scene displayed on famous Boston Common.

More recently her work has come increasingly to the notice of dog fanciers, and her bronzes particularly are in great demand for their beauty and value as collector's items. One bronze, of a Golden Retriever, is part of the collection of the Dog Museum Of America – an eloquent tribute to her ability.

She belongs to the Society of Animal Artists, the Deerfield Valley Arts Association, and the New England Antiquities Research Association. She is a Director of the Greenfield Animal Shelter and a member of several dog clubs including the prestigious Ladies' Dog Club, the venerable Boston area group.

A dog lover since childhood, Louise Shattuck's first visit to a dog show was in 1928 at the Eastern Dog Club, and that visit helped determine the shape of her future. She acquired her first dog, a parti-color American Cocker, in the 1940s and took him to his UDT title. Louise and her educated pup were an integral part of the famous New England Dog Training Club Drill Team. This dog was the first of a parade of Cockers into Louise's life all of which were obedience trained, and many also had tracking titles.

Eventually Louise was smitten with the American Cocker's English ancestor, and she remains one of the breed's staunchest supporters. The foundation matron of the Carry-On English Cockers had the tremendous distinction of earning the first UDT title for the breed. At last count, Louise's dogs have earned 22 conformation championships and a spectacular total of 73 obedience and tracking titles. Dogs of her breeding have brought pleasure to many, and some have won well for new owners both in this country and abroad. Other hobbies include horseback riding and music, although, to this last, Louise admits she can't play an instrument of any kind and perhaps she might be able to carry a tune in a wheelbarrow if she had a sturdy wheelbarrow. She is, however, a great music fan and discourses intelligently on the music of many cultures and times.

Here, Louise Shattuck tells in her own words just how it all began: "I suppose there are lots of ways people become collectors. I can never recall a time when one or another in the family weren't acquiring something. My father liked foreign coins. My aunt amassed porcelains and cloisonné, and several others pooled their efforts with Royal Doulton pitchers. Everybody bought books. Souvenir spoons were a great family tradition, as were odd silver and china. Now I am the only one left ... rattling around in a big old house ... and I have most of their collections – hell to dust, and the goal of several antique dealers. But my own taste has always run to animals. I started collecting stuffed dogs back in the dim mists of time when the family realized, sadly, that I wasn't all that keen on the dolls they lavished on me.

"At the age of reading, I began to notice animal books, dogs especially, and had to have them all! I also cut out all the dog pictures from magazines. Somewhere in the cellar to this day are a couple of cartons with who-knows-what treasures, brittle and ancient, illustrators of the 20's and 30s, probably priceless. In junior and senior high school, when it became apparent that I would follow in my mother's footsteps and attend art college, I started what every artist has to have – my 'morgue': a vast file of illustrative and reference material, mostly animal. This was the era of many of the artists and illustrators who are now revered by collectors: Charles Livingston Bull, Paul Branson (first President of the Society of Animal Artists), Marguerite Kirmse, George Ford Morris, Morgan Dennis, Paul Brown (whose dogs were as good as his famous horses) and many more.

"My first attempt at sculpture, at age 16, netted me a scholarship to college. Art school intensified the whole animal syndrome, and I spent many a day, skipping classes at times, sketching at zoos near Boston. I attended Massachusetts College of Art, as had my mother, and very quickly majored in sculpture, although in those days we learned every form of art: drawing, painting, etching and crafts. It was the greatest training for which I have always been grateful. I learned casting and mold making and upon graduation in 1941, I spent some years working at an Italian display sculpture firm, a whole experience in itself. Situated in the bowels of Boston under the elevated structure, it was a huge loft building with three floors of sculpture projects, a foot of plaster on the floor, bathtubs of clay and huge armatures where I, as resident animal sculptor, had to construct life-sized camels, sheep and cows for nativities as well as many other animals. It was cold and dirty, and no one spoke much English. The work was very physical, but it was the greatest training. Many of the craftsmen were of the old Italian school, with generations of expertise behind them. Much has been lost in this work since the war, old tools, work secrets, etc., but I still have some of the casts from my work there.

"Sketching and drawing was always a factor, and I attended my first dog show at age 8, the Eastern Dog Club show in Boston and have never missed one of their shows since except the two war years when it was canceled. Dogless I went, armed with pastels and portfolio, and stayed all day, sketching,

watching and wondering what breed I'd like to have. I went through a variety of favorites; at one time I had a passion for Afghans, and did them in every possible way."

"In the days when My Own Brucie, the famous Cocker, was the 'big noise,' I became a Cocker fan. Around 1945, just out of art school, and wanting to assert myself, I obtained my first Cocker (buff and white) and became, for life, thoroughly immersed in the dog show world. I showed this dog to the ultimate in obedience and tracking, then acquired another, and raised a litter, and the scene was set for a long over-dogged life! That dog became a UDT and traveled all over with the famous New England Dog Club's drill team. Later, I bought a black and tan; from then on, I have cast discretion to the winds and had DOGS. In time, and after much searching, I settled on the English Cocker, the original Spaniel. There wasn't much contest.

"**B**y this time, I was starting my own studios in the Boston city center. In fifteen years I had four of them in succession, old lofts where I could stir my coffee with a modeling tool and all my artist friends did too! A great time of arty fun and work. I had lots of room and no compulsion for any real decor, so up on the walls went doggy art with thumbtacks, and masses of sculpture all over, kilns, plaster easels, etc. Teaching too at that time, I did a lot of animal work with students and also taught at the old Natural History Museum and did dogs for the now long gone Contemporary Arts firm. Always I did dog portraits even back in early art school days and often wonder how many hundreds of them are out there somewhere, maybe by now moldering in attics with old Fido long gone!

"In the course of time, the studio days were over; and I inherited the family home in western Massachusetts with 13 rooms where I have spread out like creeping fungus all over. So I have spent the years in two worlds, education and teaching in Boston where four different lofts, and summers in the hills of western Massachusetts where I am now settled with an average of 10-12 dogs, several litters annually, a garden, the woods, a lake and horses. I have lost count of how many portraits I have done or how many different breeds or types of horses I have painted or sculptured. I work in pastel on sanded board I obtain in England. I have been to England about a dozen times and brought back a dog and much artwork for my own collection, Spaniels in prints, books and figurines. Over there the dog scene is at its best. For sheer variety of doggy items, there is nothing to compare with Crufts with its myriad stands of figurines and prints. I've brought back many a choice thing in my suitcase or rolled up. I have become affiliated with the firm of Heredities Ltd. in the Lake District of northern England for whom I have done a puppy series and have visited their fine plant in a lovely village. I brought back some discontinued Doris Lindner sculptures. She was, to my mind, one of the greatest dog sculptors, and recently died at age 90. With my own vast output and what I have collected, my big house is bursting. I also save every magazine having to do with dogs, horses, wildlife and the English country, as I never know when I might need a reference or inspiration.

"My work is now more and more dogs exclusively, though I still like to do other wildlife. I find that my demand comes from people who either collect their own breed or are buying perhaps in quantity for trophies. One of my most interesting and fortunate commissions was that of a field-type Golden Retriever trophy which I was asked to do by Rachel Page Elliott of *Dogsteps* fame. It had to have a bird in mouth and be running. It pleased the committee and was a success when in bronze, and a cast is in the Dog Museum of America. In portraits, I prefer heads, as opposed to show poses, as they are more soulful. In sculpture, I have had to do many odd breeds as the occasion arises, as I often have requests, usually from a club or breeder, for a breed I have to research carefully and perhaps do a large run of casts for a specialty. This is very challenging as breeders are very exacting. I have had to do Bullmastiffs, a network of wrinkles; Briards, waterfalls of hair; Portuguese Water Dogs, all curls and fuzz; and Deerhounds, all bones and angles. Each dog breed is so different. I model in plasteline and then make a rubber mold (vinyl) and cast in "cast stone" which is then bronze toned. For more pretentious pieces, I may do a one-of-a-kind fired clay stoneware sculpture, using any one of a number of high-fire clays. These pieces must be relatively compact and have to be cut apart and hollowed out before drying and firing. Clubs like these for Best of Breed or a raffle. I also have a line of pewter pins and plaques.

"My two books kept on selling steadily as new dog people get hooked on the dog game every year and discover the books; they soon find that my harried life with dogs closely approximates theirs, so they are not alone! I have always loved to do cartoons so the first two books were a natural about life with the Carry-On Cockers; they 'just happened.' They began as letters to the editor of The ECSCA Review, a national breed magazine. After a lot of articles appeared, they were published, and that was that! A fabulous lucky first time break! I feel I was enormously lucky, but it was easy writing, being based on so much happening with numerous litters, champions, obedience and tracking titles, and several champion UDT's, plus all the things that can't help but happen in that span of time.

"I have never regretted cutting life classes at art school to go to the zoo; just see what it has led to! Now, at an age where I read my contemporaries' 'obits.' I seem to be more dog-oriented than ever, learning more all the time as I study, observe, draw, sculpt and clean up after our best friends!"

Forewords

I am glad that Louise Shattuck's written work is coming to light again. Though I have long been familiar with some of the material herein, I found it hard to put down the new manuscript when it arrived for my perusal. Louise is a person who makes others happy by being herself. Life a graft on a tree she's always been there as part of my life, a privilege that I cannot put into words.

This author has a refreshing use of the English language not found in today's literature. She has an inimitable style and conveys her stories in pithy, descriptive humor, with many an incident illustrated by clever cartoons. The book may seen a bit earthy for anyone just initiated in dog ownership, but readers new and old will share many a laugh throughout. Yet there are somber, doleful interludes, where Louise talks of the inevitable losses of her beloved English Cockers, bringing to mind experiences that all of us who love animals have faced as the end of each life draws near; and it is with sensitive, poignant humor that she entwines her own indications of the on-going years with those of the "Old Dog."

To know Louise Shattuck is to feel an extension of life beyond ordinary living. Readers are in for a treat.

Rachel Page Elliott

Driving to New York for the Westminster show weekend, my wife, Betty, read out loud to me from the galleys for this, Louise Shattuck's most recent book. Intermittently throughout the long drive, she had to stop reading because she simply couldn't see through her tears of laughter. We were captivated by her vivid descriptions of such a steady stream of incidents, one after the other, describing her own life shared with her dogs and cats, that it brought back to us visions of so many of our own experiences with dogs over the years.

The text and the artwork in this latest of her literary achievements are so typical and so insightful of her own personality that it is absolutely charming from the very beginning. Louise has been the breeder extraordinaire, with all the patience in the world, and just enough of the necessary insanity to pursue her lifestyle.

Her honesty in regard to the breeding and raising of such a profusion of dogs is not only a lesson for anyone following in her footsteps to learn, but she makes every disaster into a cataclysm of comic relief, and makes them appear to be perfectly natural happenings.

Louise's sense of humor plus her artistic talents in art and creative writing are God given, gifts that are very rare in any field, but especially in the world of dogs and cats. This book is the epitome of her literary accomplishments, and should be read and savored by all.

William J. Trainor

There are a number of books on dogs, but none quite like those by Louise Shattuck. There is a remarkable understanding between her dogs and herself and she is able with her lovely sense of humor to express that understanding in her book. Despite the humorous approach there is a lot of common sense behind it all, and behind the humor the reader will get a good appreciation of how all types of situations which arise when one lives with dogs can be dealt with.

Louise is a very good artist and those models are known very well over here in England, including those shaped by her humorous outlooks, so typified by the many cartoons in her book. Browsing can be a humorous viewing of the cartoons. Reading can be a lighthearted but understanding look at the happiness and responsibilities life with dogs can bring.

George Caddy

Some years ago I helped my friend, Louise Shattuck, gather up bits and pieces of manuscript, tear sheets of cartoons and other sketches, and attempt to arrange them in some semblance of order for a somewhat unusal submission to Howell Book House. I think Louise and I were both in a state of shock when the word came back that her efforts had been accepted. It was a vicarious thrill for me too, because the start of it all had been some hilarious letters Louise had written to me back in the early 1970s when I was co-editor of our national breed club's quarterly magazine, The ECSCA Review. The original From Riches to Bitches was so successful that it "whelped" a second volume, In Stitches Over Bitches, from which some of the material in the "Pick of the Litter" has come.

So here we are again, except this time I've moved back to Wisconsin. What fun to see them again, all in one volume, so that a newer generation of dog lovers, and English Cocker fanciers in particular, can discover the never-ending saga of Louise and her "Carry-Ons" – still in there carrying on, after all these years. Enjoy!

Kate D. Romanski

I.
The Sub-Culture

With dogs one manages to rise above almost any eventuality if one is in any kind of balance; however, one's balance often teeters. Such a situation cropped up recently. I have fairly successfully weeded out all non-doggy-oriented friends, and it hasn't been too hard because they tend to depart by choice. However, an old friend of many years turned up not too long ago and renewed old times in my fur-lined living room. He and his wife had attended a championship celebration party I'd given previously, and I realized then how one really MUST NOT include non-doggy people at such events. The whole thing is such a foreign element to them, as they sit sipping their Scotch, edging away from pink tongues and furry faces bent on snatching an hors d'oeuvre. Everyone else is up to the eyeballs with the "in" jargon: bitches in heat, stud dog services, worms, stools, eczema, vet bills, disinfectants, retained placentas, and of course, wins, judges, shows and what AKC says.

The Protest

Here she comes — every week — with her masses of hair shirts...

The Sub-Culture

The classic remark ... and the ONLY remark from my non-doggy friends as I recall ... came during a rare lull – "Why, it's a whole SUB-CULTURE!" And indeed it is, as I am the first to acknowledge.

Anyway, braving the fur people again, sat my old acquaintance calling on some totally non-doggy business. It has been said that people who don't like cats were rats in their last incarnation. I wonder what non-doggers were, possibly cats. Anyway, non-doggers are always reasonably polite, trying to ignore the multiple canines or, at worst, coming up with a sickly smile. Maintaining one's poise is rather difficult when boisterous English Cockers do their thing, which means appear as objectionable as possible, leap about, smell pants, catapult onto chairs and couches like boomerangs, bark deafeningly in

unison, drop ancient bones on guests' toes, and shake hair all about while trotting endlessly hither and yon.

The best thing, of course, is to corral them all, protesting loudly, and shut them in the kitchen; but then one pays the price by conversing above the door-scratching, howls, and noise of the overturned-trash hunt.

So one tends to tolerate, as dog persons are so thoroughly inured to all such peccadilloes that generally there is little recognition of the guest's state of mind. On this occasion, Kelpie (UDT, yet), never ill in her life, chose to take the spotlight by first planting herself in my guest's lap, looking soulfully into his face, and calmly throwing up untold quantities of second-hand Purina on his jacket and down the side of the chair. Hopping down, she repeated the performance in several more choice spots on the rug and finished off with a rousing crescendo of gagging and more Purina on the couch.

This is where even the doggy hostess' "cool" cracks. WHAT can be done but profuse apologies, much arm waving, and banishing the culprit, who by now is feeling fine and ready for more Purina. Then begins the grisly job with paper towels and bucket. Meanwhile, the guest surveys the wreckage of his haberdashery and looks green.

This is indeed the sub-culture! One gets totally used to such cleaning tasks, but non-doggy persons display a horror of the whole episode akin to visiting a leper colony, which is about what they privately think of your household anyway. For OTHER evidence along the way also has made a pretty poor impression, such as a cat sitting on the stove dipping into a pan (a clever trick not perfected by many cats, but not generally seen in the life of a non-anamalier either). Also, not many anti-creature people would understand a dog grubbing about in the kitty litter box, but there's one in every family. And a fine film of animal hair tending to collect in balls in well-traveled areas doesn't go over well with neat-freaks.

The non-doggy guest has just about disappeared from my life, thanks be; but on such rare occasions, you just know it's the guest's room where bones or the old squirrel tail are brought, and the canine with the "summer itch" spends hours thumping the floor outside the insomniac's door. Late sleepers are discouraged due to the din of the crated members, singing a hymn to the dawn like canine Valkyries.

How much more welcome are the guests with various canines of their own! They arrive brisk and jolly and nerveless, laden with crates, dog food, liver, vitamins, tack boxes, old boots, and tolerance.

Well, it's all chalked up to experience, and I must say, "Long live the Sub-Culture!"

The Dog Fancier's Telephone Marathon

Overheard by a flea on the wall in the average dog breeder's home: The feminine partner is on the phone ... endlessly, settled down for a good "natter" as they say in Ireland, and the masculine half is off to one side, hovering about, kibitzing, or in a chair, and long suffering.

"Yes, that's true; but you know I always say, you can't really tell if it's the bitch's fault or the stud's, and after eight litters the Dewlaps' kennel has had a total of thirty-seven major defects, and now Cornell has asked them to write up a paper on it, and still they claim it's the stud's fault, not THEIR bitches, and they've used a zillion different studs, so what can you think ... GEORGE! That dog is on the table. WATCH IT! Well, never mind; the

The Sub-Culture

peanuts are all gone now, but she always throws them up, so watch her ... Yes, Sylvia, I'm here. Oh! Is that so? How awful. Oh, George, guess what! Tom's champion has just swallowed the dental tape container and he's taking it to the vet on an emergency trip ... OH GEORGE! ... Yes, Sylvia, George thinks it's awful, too, but he says he always did think that dog had teeth in it's ... Oh, well, you know how George talks. OH! Is that so? The Cowhocks have gone out of dogs!? Well, it's about time after THEIR specimens ... remember that AWFUL bitch ... oh, they've sold her? Well, she really was a mess ... WHAT!? She just got a five-point major! Under who? HIM? Why, even his contact lenses are old! Well, it takes all kinds ... GEORGE, check the outside dogs! ... Yes, Sylvia, I'm here. Two of the dogs are back to digging again. They've just uncovered our septic tank ... It's the pits ... Oh, you're having trouble breeding that bitch? Join the club! Yes, I sure do know how it is! A houseful of nothing but bitches, and every one has joined Gay Liberation! Those intense relationships with each other and the cats ... yep, sometimes several at a clip, real daisy chains, wall-to-wall sex ... but send them off to the stud at a wild fee and you know how it is ... sudden SHY VIRTUE ... 'Don't come near me, you rapist!' and all that hard to get stuff. (Shut up, George, we're talking about DOGS) ... yes, but you know owning the stud can be difficult too, of course; how about that young one who has to have a darkened room and soft music, and if anyone appears he just goes off and studies his toenails indifferently ... I think he was scolded for some juvenile peccadillo and has a guilt complex ... NO, GEORGE! NOT you! We're still on dogs! We are NOT talking dirty! Dogs aren't EVER dirty, only people! ... Go off and read your *Playboy*, why don't you? Or run out in the kitchen and investigate that clattering ... it may be the roast ... if it is, we eat out tonight. Yes, Sylvia, I'm here. Oh, did you read that article in the *Enquirer* about Lolita Liplure?

Her husband is suing for divorce for having 18 dogs in their bedroom! Imagine! How cruel and callous! (SHUT UP, GEORGE! You know we have only seven and no more of your snide cracks either.) Well, I always say anyone all that fond of dogs can't be all bad even if she IS a sex symbol. I think she's gotten to the age where dogs are replacing sex anyway. (GEORGE! Save those remarks for your bar friends! GEORGE! Why don't you go out and practice with that new pooper scooper you got for your birthday? DO SOMETHING ... don't stand there heckling!) Yes, Sylvia, George got the nicest things for his birthday, much nicer than what he'd been asking for, stuff like golf clubs and booze. I found this new type jumbo pooper scooper with a special padded handle, very fancy with Early American designs, and I told his sister to get him a set of aluminum feeding pans, so easy to clean, and the children all gave him knitted snoods for the dogs, and some great new kennel disinfectant in Olde Spice! Oh, he had a great birthday even if the dogs DID eat his cake ... yes, he seemed pleased ... or that is, as much as he ever is, you know how he is, that muffled voice coming out of the big chair under layers of dogs ... GEORGE? Are you back? Where are you? Speak up! Are you in the chair? All I see is the dogs ... GEORGE ... speak to me ... wave your handkerchief ... GEORGE ... is that your slipper down there with you in it or just a dog toy? Well, Sylvia, I THINK George is in the chair again, but there are ten dogs on top so you really can't tell. He may be dozing, but then again he may be having one of his charley-horse cramps so I'd better go dig him out ... see if he's breathing ... One of the dogs is chewing on something that may be his hair, and he has little enough, heaven knows! Yes, Sylvia, I'll talk to you later. I've got some hot news about the Ovabans. I hear they're on the verge of a divorce and fighting over the custody of the dogs; they each want them, but neither of them wants the kids ... ALL RIGHT, GEORGE ... I'm coming! Dogs! Supper-supper!"

Gripes and Grumbles of the Grooming Game

Many things are far from ideal about owning and operating a grooming shop, and this is in spite of the gratification that comes of sending home a smart looking canine in the afternoon that arrived a walking mop that morning.

Every day brings its little traumas and memorable episodes. There was the time a very longhaired girl kept a tight grip on her dog while I worked

the clutcher

on the nails with the grinding attachment on the A2 clipper. Most dogs react to this operation with every trick in the book short of schizophrenia. This time the struggle led to the attachment catching the owner's flowing tresses and a SUPER SNARL. Of course, nails were immediately abandoned, and it took an hour and some regrettable scissor work to make amends.

I also remember the large woman who insisted on staying with her tiny Toy Poodle during the entire grooming operation. She hovered over the grooming table as well as the dog, totally obscuring him from view, let alone reach, with her enormous bosom. And all the while she would admonish him in Polish to be good while he snapped, growled and otherwise threatened nastily. Every three minutes she would repeat the same baleful admonition, "Be careful of his little peanut!"

The sandbag dog is a fairly common phenomenon. This is the pooch who is not unusually heavy, but becomes akin to 100 pounds of cement when placed on the grooming table. Characteristically, the sandbag dog must be propped, prodded and poked to rise at all as he clutches the table surface, grimly immovable. Even the simplest grooming operations become major tactical maneuvers when you face this type. He's good for working off your extra calories, though.

Another noteworthy challenge is the whirling dervish dog. A moving target in every sense, this type is another well represented in my hairy clientele. The whirling dervish is hard on your grooming equipment and your back. In the first instance, this dog keeps knocking combs, brushes and scissors into the farthest reaches of the grooming room as it spins madly around on the table. The continued free-flight episodes can't do your gear a bit of good. And the need to continuously retrieve them eventually tells on your sacroiliac.

There are always those fat dogs I must heave to the tub by main force, feeling the birth of a double hernia throughout. In contrast are the tiniest Poodles and other very small Toys you are sure will disintegrate in your grasp if you use anything stronger than a gossamer touch. The undaunted flea is the only reason many dogs are ever brought to a groomer.

Many affected unfortunates have found their sad way to Carry-On, and their zillion fleas successfully hopped off enroute to the dipping tub. The dog got clean; and the fleas escaped certain doom at the last minute, only to inhabit my home forever.

I'm getting to the point of dreading an encounter with a small dog on a summer day. Invariably, this little fellow comes when I have all doors and windows open; at the VERY FIRST tentative, gentle touch of the brush, he starts a truly shattering session of ear-splitting shrieking and yelping. The blood-curling recital is so vivid, you're sure the whole neighborhood is on the phone to the SPCA to have YOU taken away.

And just about my only total failure was the ten-year-old Scotty/Peke cross. Although super matted, he came in amiable and seemed rather absent-minded until the clipper sliced away a wide swath of filthy, matted hair. At this outrage, the old crossbred was transformed into a raging lion ready, willing and entirely able to put teeth into his side of the argument. Too tough even for me, he departed shortly afterward, never to return but with a unique trim – one wide swath right down the back!

Owners are often as trying as the dogs, and sometimes more so. Many haven't the slightest notion of how their genetically dubious dogs should be trimmed, and leave it up to me, saying "use your own judgment." Such a one comes back to collect his pet, and upon discovering the absence of the two-year-old, rock-hard, matted beard I gladly severed, moans, "Oh, he doesn't look like Benji anymore!"

Some owners think you can make bricks without straw. These are the ones who bring pictures of adorable shaggy dogs cut out of magazine ads or children's books, asking that you trim their virtually hairless, mangy-looking "Heinz" to "look just like that."

Anyone who grooms for others has experienced the grossly inconsiderate person who leaves a dog with you, promising to return on the dot of noon. Of course, this owner doesn't return for Rover all day, and Rover reacts accordingly. He spends the whole afternoon barking in his crate, fouls himself not once, but TWICE, ruins his fresh trim and is a psycho wreck when the owner finally does arrive at 5:00 p.m. with a flimsy excuse.

I get particularly bitter over owners with large, hairy dogs that come on very rainy days. It's not unusual for these clients to allow their dogs a leisurely, fifteen minute browse before entering the grooming room. After the dog has relieved itself all over the place, you are left to cope with a wringing wet coat requiring a long drying session before you even get to begin the real grooming.

There seems no end to human effrontery where dog grooming visits are concerned. I've had a whole family, mother and four small kids come in with young Poopsie for her first trim. They must stay awhile so the kids can see Poopsie getting her first haircut and the inevitable result is near pandemonium. Grappling with panicky Poopsie (who has been brought in on a horse chain) is enough for two people. But by now the kids, with quixotic changes of interest, are spraying each other with any aerosols in reach, dumping grooming powder on the floor, and beating each other with slicker brushes; one has begun to climb into the bathtub. I have no luck. Mother believes in allowing full child expression so chastises no one. Poopsie fouls the grooming table and ultimately escapes under the oil tank. I'll spare you the rest.

My grooming room, like grooming rooms everywhere, is coated with a film of grooming powder. A pall of various sprays hangs always in the air. Therefore, I am constantly haunted by thoughts centering on the state of my lungs and nasal passages. The furnace man comes regularly to clean and service the furnace which happens to be near the grooming table. He always makes it a point to show me the mass of hair and gunk he collects from the innards of the heating plant. If a cast iron furnace can be clogged to that extent, I dread to contemplate the state of my own inner workings.

But as with most things, there is usually a pattern. The owner arrives and for half an hour discloses all the little foibles and idiosyncrasies of the victim. He warns against a variety of imaginary phobias, the presence of minute warts, and sheepishly admits that "he snaps a little, sometimes." Having given all the caveats, owner departs; and when dog and groomer are safely alone, I become pack leader, using all the time-worn tricks I've picked up from books I've read on the subject of the pack leader syndrome. No more Mr. Good Guy for this groomer. Discipline reigns, and after a few eyeballing sessions and a little physical reinforcement, if it can't be helped, a miracle happens. Almost every cantankerous canine settles down deciding here finally is someone, unlike the owner, who cannot be bamboozled. Harmony ensues and by the time the owner comes to get the dog, things have become very amicable. The

The totally dog oriented person...

owner seems quite surprised to find that there was no bloodshed on either side and all is serene. This is the reward of being a pack leader. Somehow it has yet to work on my own dogs who acknowledge NO leader. It's every man for himself, and the best man is the one who reaches the refrigerator FIRST!

Tell Me What You Drive and I'll Tell You What You Are

At one stage or another of dog show devotion (addiction?), most fanciers' vehicles tend to become billboards attesting to the owners' passions for one form or another of canine competition. This encompasses the contents of the typical wagon, car, van or RV, as well as the buggy itself.

Crates, essential to the operation of the serious enthusiast, are ever present. They have even been jammed into the backseat of the venerable VW bug as need dictated. Crates are available in many styles and can often be observed piled upon one another inside not too large autos in unbelievable numbers and equally incredible arrangements. Like some styles of ladies' shoes, some autos must be built small on the outside and large on the inside and many are in demand for dog shows.

Special accessories for the dog person's car proliferate. Their use and demand depend on the season of the year and the part of the country. When the sun beats down, some people use space-age type screening devices so the dogs keep their cool. In northern climes, or when dog shows happen during deep winter, snug sheepskin rugs provide an extra measure of welcome warmth enroute.

If the dog person's conveyance is not a van or an RV, an adequate roof rack is a must. The roof rack is a natural for carrying dollies, exercise pens, tables and collapsed wire crates; and all of these IMPERATIVE items are lashed to the rack with yards and yards of the special elastic cords made for this purpose.

Watching the cars and vans unload is like watching the famous old act in the Shriners parade where about fifty midgets keep emerging from a tiny car in a totally unbelievable way. What comes out of these cars is just as unbelievable as the amount of gear disgorged. From the look of things, some owners must work with complicated blueprints and floor plans drawn up far in advance to accommodate the staggering amount of equipment used. The need to get every essential INTO a vehicle to take to the show, OUT of the vehicle to use at the show, and IN again prior to the return trip brings out unbelievable strains of fanciers' ingenuity as packers. This ability is even more dramatic when one considers that the loading, unloading and reloading are almost always accomplished without losing one's place, a dog or two, or some valuable piece of equipment.

What is most intriguing, however, is not what goes INTO a dog person's rig, but what goes ON IT! One often sees spare tire compartments on vans sporting enormous oil paintings of a favorite dog, a clever motto, or the

The Sub-Culture

owner's kennel name. Usually they are a bit worse off from the road wear gathered on trips to a zillion dog shows, but they are still startling. Some vans and wagons are emblazoned with the kennel name or a favorite slogan in large letters on both sides! Wait, there's more. There has to be a Snoopy on the dashboard and as many bumper stickers as can be made to fit. It matters not that there are only so many inches of bumper to accommodate these earth-shaking messages. Stick 'em all over.

A dog car's exterior ornamentation runs to incredible lengths. One notes endless numbers of stickers advising the world that the occupants of this car belong to at least seventeen specialty clubs for THEIR breed from Alaska to South Florida and a few local all-breed clubs for good measure. Many also proclaim their membership in a couple or so obedience clubs and, for Sporting breed people, membership in one or more field trial clubs is also proclaimed via the bumper sticker route. Those with cosmopolitan leanings include graphic evidence of membership in a few clubs for their breed from various foreign countries.

Bumper stickers also work out well as warnings and proclamations. Examples of the former might include the admonition that the car in front of you carries show dogs, so don't tailgate, that the driver always brakes for small animals, or that the dogs within are tattooed through an established registry.

Proclamation bumper stickers tell the onlooker that the owner of this rolling billboard is opposed to traps, seal clubbing, wearing fur, eating meat, and the use of DDT. Furthermore, the highminded altruist is for saving whales, dolphins, and the hog-nosed turtle. He or she, like Smokey the Bear, is always careful about forest fires, and ALWAYS spays and neuters. Other messages one sees ask if you have hugged your dog today, tell you that happiness is a whatever breed the driver has, and that it's great to be of whatever ethnic background the driver is. That's far from the limit as the inventive wits that labor in the idea tanks of wherever bumper stickers are created are constantly bringing about more to tantalize.

Some are so priceless that they must be stuck on the car even though there's no more room except on the windshield. Some examples include these I've seen, smiled at, and can't find where to buy: "Rottweilers Do It On Command"; "Obedience Trainers Do It With Both Hands"; "Poodles Do It In French"; "Dachsies Do It The Long Way"; "Dog Groomers ... (well, I'll delete that one as this is a family book), or maybe "Huskies Do It In Snow." I really should have a bumper sticker made up for my dogs – "Carry-On Cockers Do It On Rugs"– a new twist perhaps, but less likely to be X-rated.

Anyway, there it is; a car is a symbol of one's ruling passion. At least as the caravan of showbound autos speeds by, ever behind schedule, other motorists on the highway can gasp and say to their passengers, "Wow! Did you read THAT car?"

Some Hidden Nasties of Dog Life

Sometimes you just feel contemptible thinking about things that happen that somehow take the spiritual quality out of the doggy life. After administering tapeworm pills and hanging around all day for some action, one leaves for a quick trip to shop for a guest. You know that the arrival of the guest will coincide with tapeworming results as the atmosphere mutely testifies.

Garlic buds are said to be efficacious for flea control, but they render the whole house a pizza palace as you enter, not to mention what they do to your hands.

For several cold late fall nights, a last lingering blue bottle fly had zoomed about my room in final spurts of failing energy, determined, like Dylan Thomas' poem, not to "go gentle into that good night" of fly oblivion! The bed Cocker snapped valiantly over and over in a vain attempt to send the insect on faster to its destiny ... thus disturbing my precious bedtime reading (old *Gazettes*) ... that marvelous midnight siesta with a glass of juice and good doggy books! Every dog-snap shattered the tranquillity, not to mention the leaps over the prostrate human form. After some time of this irritating performance, the whole thing took a nasty turn, totally unexpected, and not to the satisfaction of the Cocker, me, or the fly. In one last buzzing display of aerial technique, it fell inadvertently into my juice and I drank him.

What's got to be the pits was a tale I heard at a dog show ... some ill-fated person whose stars were probably all wrong for that day was in the port-a-potty with his LARGE DOG TIED TO THE OUTSIDE HANDLE, only to have that the occasion when said large dog challenged a passing fellow dog, rocking the port-a-potty off its moorings, and catching the occupant helplessly off-guard.

For six months I've had another insect problem, little small moths flitting about the kitchen; and, of course, I was SURE they were clothes moths after my woolens. But, no. After I'd hand-swatted a few million, someone told me they were common grain moths, coming out of old cereal boxes ... or ... more likely, dog meal. Nothing has stemmed the tide so far, no matter how much I have searched, so it is to be presumed they are in the walls practicing population explosion on Purina.

You never know what pitfalls lurk in the doggy life. One of my dog club acquaintances with too many dogs for the size of her house, bed, and wallet has taken to "closet drinking." Recently, a dog leaped up joyously as she

was tilting the gin bottle to mouth and broke off her front tooth.

How many oldster dogs had the summer itch this past year and flaunted their runny sores like a leper colony to visitors new to the breed who had come to look over the "beautiful English Cockers ... "

I think behavior researchers might do a study of the human john habits. Who knows what the john occupant REALLY observes, being in a sort of special state of limbo? But I can attest that they DON'T read lids! Be they young, old, with or without glasses, short or tall, they NEVER close lids . . . and the English Cockers continue, as always, to slurp from the john. I am resigned to following after guests and closing lids myself, snarling. I have had a vigorous campaign going for over a year and have chalked up 100% failure. I spent hours of great artistry painting pleas on my seat covers (BOTH of them!) with carefully flourished calligraphy that shouts, hopefully, to the startled eyes of the user: "PLEASE CLOSE LID! ROTTEN DOGS LIVE HERE!" followed by a pattern of painstakingly painted pawprints wandering around in an oval like a vine tendril. The inner seat, for gents, has an even more strident message. But it's no use. Just the same with the kitty litter box, which the cockers LOVE ... but that's too gross to even mention ...

II.
Days of Our Lives

Recollections of the Festive Spirit and Holiday Joys at Carry-On

At Christmas, homes with multitudinous children or dogs must certainly be the ultimate in stress, strain, strife and celebration. The over-doggy house has no peer for all-out confusion at this joyous time.

The Carry-Ons, including the cats, sense Christmas long before one is really into shopping and mail-order catalogs. Each critter hones up nose, ears, claws, and teeth, as well as wits. As the pile of presents accumulates in the spare room, the humans steadily lose the yearly struggle to keep them intact until Christmas Day.

Starting well in advance of Christmas, I plan craftily to avoid all the previous years' disasters, so all packages go into a guest room, high up on bed and bureau. Since most friends and relatives send gaily wrapped dog goodies, these have never made it to Christmas Eve, nor have boxes of candy, soft slippers or squeaky toys. Each year, by some means, the fur people manage to infiltrate the treasure room, perhaps when I enter, one hiding under the bed as I leave and shut the door. Later, of course, I discover packages opened, bows unraveled, edibles devoured, ad nauseam. It's an old story, a broken record.

This was the fifth straight year clever Crispy demolished most of the special chocolate butterscotch. She and some of her apprentice Mafia also accounted for some leather gloves the day after their purchase. A jar of apricot brandy sauce was saved just in time as the culprit pulled off the wrappings and was discovered prying off the lid. Special English soap appears to be a favorite. One bar of violet was opened four times, sampled, rewrapped, and finally met its giftee in sad state.

Delicacies from distant relatives, such as boxes of glacé fruits, smoked beef sausage, cheese samplers, candy and nuts are real hazards and must be removed immediately. But the real problem is that they arrive festively wrapped so who is to know what the contents are; the answer: the Cockers. THEY know and will act surreptitiously, only opening the edibles when no one is about. Perhaps you've closed the spare room door with a slam, and put a chair under the knob, and are off to a party or concert, something jolly and uplifting and seasonal. Without a doubt, homecoming undoes all the holiday spirit when telltale wreckage leads you to the carnage. Or maybe you're listening to the season's sixth presentation of *Messiah* on TV, with several dogs, like angels, on the couch. Your joy to the world is shattered when the crash

occurs, and you leap upstairs to find clever Kelpie running off, trailing ribbon, a bow in her ear, chomping the rabbit fur slippers.

Several of the dogs have gotten into the spice jar set (another Christmas gift) and spilled garlic powder all over the rug. Each one shared the tasty job of cleaning it all up delightedly, leaving the festive room no longer redolent of pine hearth fire and roasting turkey. Each dog then greeted guests all day with ecstatic leaps and kisses, breathing heavy garlic breath on all those unfortunate enough to be in their proximity.

During the Christmas Eve gift unwrapping, the problem is who to exclude. Certainly not the 15-year-old who, it is certain, will see no more such times. Nor can you exclude the several youngsters who are ecstatic over the thrill of their first Christmas. And the middle-aged ones, starting to settle down into some semblance of post-pregnant propriety, certainly should not be banished to the crates. The oldster, so tottery, is sure to piddle on the presents, since she can't be trusted; and the youngest ones are sure to piddle on the presents because THEY can't be trusted. The middle-aged ones will take this opportunity to cleverly sneak out to the kitchen in case there are unguarded refreshments to be had, or go about filching people's egg nogs surreptitiously. At least one young one will eat an unshelled Brazil nut, and another will upchuck a batch of Christmas tree needles all over a present.

Activity abounds during gift opening as English Cockers fan out so as to cover all phases of the action. One grubs in the remaining unopened gifts; another spirits a hickory smoked cheese under a chair; another shreds paper and bows; and yet another laps up someone's egg nog. Clever Crispy makes a solo foray to the kitchen in case some hapless edible goodies can be reached or the oven door pried open.

The new kitten, hysterical at his first Christmas, has disappeared into the paper bag of discarded bows and ribbons and nearly gets thrown away. He escapes in time to run up the Christmas tree, dislodging some heirloom Austrian ornaments which shatter and are, naturally, crunched up by the nearest dog.

From the California relatives' Christmas box came assorted incense sticks in exotic fragrances. It would strain your credulity to learn one was labeled "Chocolate Cake." So help me, Gospel. But no one is surprised to hear that this package was the only fragrance chewed up, leaving small, twig-like sticks which evaded the vacuum for weeks.

The Christmas tree is in for great attention from all members who are experiencing their first Christmas. Despite the greatest vigilance, the casualties are many. Ornaments are jarred off and crunched. Tinsel is continuously pulled off. One knows it is REALLY Christmas when, out with the pooper-scooper, the stools are found to be woven through with tinsel.

Pandemonium, of course, reigns throughout the entire gift opening, with humans arguing heatedly the pros and cons of putting all dogs in crates and enduring their howls of rage, or being one-armed paper hangers, grabbing at gifts and goodies and drinks and salvaging whatever possible. Half the gifts which have been stored have that second-hand look, having been tampered with anyway. Only after midnight, when the scene recalls the aftermath of *Star Wars,* does the pace slacken. That's when everyone mentions in wonderment the phenomenon of ALL dogs and cats asleep, totally sacked out before the hearth, like an old-time English Christmas card. It is a moment of peace and total awe. Every animal is replete, as are the humans. There is talk of getting out the cameras and chronicling this rare moment, but no one has the pizzazz. It won't last long anyway as all will be up in violent animation, with a second wind, when it's finally crate time with the goodnight Christmas chewies. By this time every squeaky toy will have had the squeaky removed and swallowed. Before everyone is relegated to the crates, several valuable gifts will be found nibbled and gnawed under chairs.

Someone mentioned that poinsettias are poisonous, so during the holidays one or another human was forever removing a frond from dogs or cats, while the plants become gradually denuded; and the new kitten dug a potty hole in the soil of the biggest one.

FINALLY on Christmas Day, we attempt the great feat in true English tradition. This is a time for great hardness of heart, kenneling them all while the bird is stuffed, and listening to their wails. The cats must go too, as they are insane with joy at the prospect of giblets to gnaw. For days after, it is a battle of wits to make a safari to the refrigerator for a turkey snack since every fourfootie is immediately there, thrusting nose and tongue in ahead of you.

And they are all acutely aware that the carcass will eventually be picked clean and disposed of. No spot is safe. The trash bags and barrels are to be guarded vigorously until the trash collection day, for nothing delights a Cocker more than to gain possession of all or part of a turkey corpse. What bliss!

Some Holiday Dinner tips might go as follows:

1. Do not invite non-doggy guests. 2. Do not invite dog-lovers who slip goodies to dogs under the table. 3. Do not invite guests who bring dogs.

Solution: Do not invite guests. Eat out.

And also – get champagne without corks. Corks fly, and dogs eat corks, and corks cork up dogs. Ditto dates with pips, candied figs and holly berries; all are sure to call for the remedy that binds.

I once envisioned myself as a sort of reincarnated English country squire in front of my fireplace, sipping my port, faithful spaniels at my feet, and all that sort of thing.

I now have the fireplace, the port, and the spaniels, but somehow the original picture doesn't hang together. I am far more likely to be on my knees before the fireplace either mopping up my spilled port or a puppy puddle, my finger ends disintegrating from too much Pine-Sol.

After the last festive days, clean-up time is another great occasion for revelry among the fur people who face it all with high spirits, unlike the holiday-jaded humans. Dry Christmas tree needles cling to ears endlessly, as well as bits of holly and twigs. Ornaments and tinsel are found in dog beds well into February.

The trips up the attic stairs to put away the decorations are accompanied by whichever dogs bully their way past the laden humans, and there are always several enterprising canines and numerous cats which make it to the unfinished attic, forbidden territory. The cats scurry off to the dark and secret corners under the eaves in search of game, and the dogs blunder and upset and disturb the dust and discarded treasures of three generations, never heeding your screams.

One clever one has discovered a long-dead mouse in great-grandfather's bedpan, while another explorer has attacked the old dressmaker's dummy ferociously; and still another has found and chewed a rare old Civil War book, the sale of which could have financed your next trip to Crufts.

Once it's all past, and every vestige of the festive season is over, I mentally clear the decks for the American Spaniel Club show, Westminster, and spring. This is the time at last for resolutions and, as the hippie said, "Getting my act together, man."

For gaining the upper hand in the canine department, buy a new industrial vacuum that REALLY gets up dog hair. Find an attachment that picks up chewed broom straws. Write to DuPont for a super air freshener spray that REALLY prevents visitors from guessing you ever had a doggy accident. Find a soundproof crate cover. Train them all to stop barking at my mental ESP command. Raise all beds, chairs and couches by two feet at least ... well, these are only some of the dreams for the New Year. For the first practical step, I shall buy some emetic from the druggist against the day when the Christmas litter of puppies discovers the house and its multitude of swallowable foreign bodies. Possibly one pup may stay to enjoy next year's holidays, a first Christmas with all its delights.

As plans are made for the year ahead, a brief glance over the canine "horrorscopes" might be in order. Examination shows that ALL dogs in the house were born on adverse days, with the Moon under Mars, which everyone KNOWS is rotten. The year ahead poses problems, one sees at a glance, for fur folk.

Starting the first week it says: Monday. "Expect news from a distance." (Half your entries at the Spaniel show got there too late.) "Guard against lack of cooperation with a mate." (Your stud dog is sulking or has gone odd and won't breed that special bitch.) Tuesday. "Some financial setbacks today!" (Your vet has sent his worst bill yet, and several furry friends need immediate medical attention.) "Long-range plans may need altering!" (Your champion bitch didn't take, so that special litter is only a pipe dream.) Wednesday. "Travel to distant places may pose problems." (Enroute to the Spaniel show, your dogs mess their crates, and one eats his leash, and you arrive too late for your reserved rooms and are established at a flophouse motel nine miles away.) Thursday. "Venus in opposition to Saturn which may indicate stalemates." (Your dog has chewed the bedspread, and you arrive too late for your class. Later you find the dog has eaten the horrorscope and thrown it up, now unintelligible. Just as well.)

Next Christmas, by the way, I have on my list of resolutions a good starter: Send all dogs to boarding kennel, and visit non-doggy relative who raises tropical fish. And so on for the New Year.

Things to Be Thankful For in the Post-Holiday Season

In spite of the fact that my four-footed terrorists never even slow down for the holidays (usually they speed up), I find myself happy for what I have when the festive season is past. And every year it seems, I have more blessings to count. Well, I consider them blessings. In the post-Holiday season I can be grateful:

... that the pumpkin pie I set far back on the counter, safe from the longest English Cocker tongue and most dexterous English Cocker paw, remained (reasonably) edible. However, the Siamese cat took a few experimental laps, found it unacceptable, and went off, walking through it.

... and that the same Siamese is still in reasonably good repair since he has just about perfected his technique of going almost anywhere in a twelve-room house without touching the floor. Slipping from surface to surface topside, like Tarzan, he thus avoids avid kisses and pummeling from the doggy horde.

... that the pre-Christmas gift depredations, a Carry-On tradition, were (comparatively) minimal since a screening technique eliminated all edibles, wrapped or unwrapped from the guest room cache. One exception: a round, tin box with colored pictures of Prince Charles and Princess Diana on the lid, which held (we think) fruit-filled candy. This was plucked from a vast pile of nonedibles, the cellophane and lid removed, and all candy consumed. No one had a glimpse of the crime. Happily, the likenesses of the Royal couple emerged from the ordeal unscathed.

... that the bean bag chair has been revitalized after years of invisible, slow leaks of its microscopic white beads, difficult and virtually impossible to vacuum up. Toenail holes are to blame. A day's work bee with vinyl plastic repair kits served to plug up the holes after much larger plastic beads were stuffed in to plump out the previously limp form. Now much firmer, the bean bag chair is not as concave, and so not as adaptable to the bodies of four or five dogs pretzelled into a clot in its depths, but a boon to the more agile human guests who favor it for a fireside perch.

Now it is like a mountain, with as many as six dogs perched on its sides and one lucky one gracing the pinnacle much like a mountaineer who has made it to the top of Everest. But one episode, best forgotten, in the checkered career of our bean bag chair, happened on a snowy night of sub-zero weather, as the aftermath of a cozy Carry-On photo session. The chair had been moved directly in front of the blazing hearth with all the dogs reclining upon it and blended into one vast, furry mound. As the dogs blissfully soaked up the heat, and the flash camera dutifully recorded all the precious poses, no one noticed what the unusually hot fire was doing to the chair. Someone had put an extra log on the fire and herein lay the grievous flaw. To our communal horror, the chair became welded to the firescreen occasioning grief on a number of fronts.

Cooked vinyl smells rotten, and to this day the firescreen bears a patch of frizzled green vinyl where the bonding came to be. In all likelihood that patch, no matter how reduced, will always be there. Prying chair and fire screen apart resulted in a monster crack in the former's roasted surface and the escape of a GOODLY supply of the tiny beads. Some were roasted. Others, full of static electricity and glad to escape, scampered to the far corners of the room to show up the next year. A large number were eaten by the puppies and were later recycled in Nature's master plan, and several blue roans wore tiny white beads in their ears and feathers for days. The repaired burn is now at the bottom of the chair, probably weakened and ready to give way any day now.

... and then I'm grateful that the four-month-old apprentice hellion who is seeing her first winter has confined gnawing to the less lush, more inexpensive plants, praise be. Thus far, she has only chewed one electrical cord irreparably, although the carrying case for the slide projector will see service no more, ditto several of the boxes of my best slides of Scotland. Yet, YET it's a small price to pay for a marked improvement in midnight howling, hiding car keys, and chewing up vital pages of dog magazines, all habits of a few weeks ago.

... and I'm also grateful that I'm finally having some success with a typed list of 100 alliterative names for puppies to give to each puppy buyer. I bother with the list at all in an attempt to reduce the possibility of innocent

From Riches to Bitches

dogs being registered with horrendous names I can't bear to repeat. The only notable exception is a dear orange roan who went to a professor and was named *Sigmund Freud* – what a blow! I must psychoanalyze that one.

... that I finally discovered a dry-cleaning shop that WILL get dog hairs off my best velour shirt and velveteen blazer at less than the initial price of the garments themselves. Of course, the shop is in a town some distance from home, and the round trip requires a tank of gas. The people there also take forever to do the work, but they don't do badly even if they don't get all the drool off the sleeves!

... if someone ever invents a *time-release bone* or *chewie*. With such a scientific marvel, I could give the dogs their nighttime treat to keep them occupied until they think they've finished and drifted off to sleep. Then, in the morning, when the Carry-On choristers get busy in preparation for the dawn ritual of howling me out of bed ... voila! The time-release agent activates more chewable material, and the dogs' attention is turned again to their treasures. Their renewed occupation gives me the pleasure of a few more precious moments of delicious sleep.

Yes, for all these things, real or imagined, I can be very grateful, indeed.

Cooking with Whips

Let me explain and clarify. It has been impossible, what with the increase of HOUSE dogs, to either get THEIR supper or MINE without the use of a whip. I buy the el cheapo ones at the tack shop, leather riding crops which soon become shreds, chewed up or broken.

I do not use them to WHIP DOGS ... I haven't stooped to that yet, though am sometimes sorely tempted. I use them to whack the metal surfaces of the stove, fridge or sink in resounding bangs to deter the dogs from leaping on me, snatching the food, clawing up my legs, grabbing things in my hand, etc.

"What?" an alert reader may ask, "Don't your obedience dogs all sit quietly in a row while you're busy?" Far from it. This they may do in class and sometimes in dog shows, but never at home. The "sit-on-command" and "stay-till-I-tell-you" are only done by genius intelligent Border Collies who have a built-in human brain and never need a lesson.

"Why don't you crate them while you cook?" someone might ask (foolishly). Because they can all do scent discrimination and can smell a bird a mile away, so crating in the basement is no solution. The faintest aroma of food wafts down to let them know culinary arts are afoot. Bedlam is the result.

A reader may recoil in horror . . . "You use whips with your dogs! Intimidation!" No. They never get whipped. More often they grab the whip

and pull and shred it. The stove, counters and fridge don't fight back, so they get it as I brandish it while yelling "Down!" "NO!" "Off!" Actually, it's not a perfect solution, but it helps a little and serves to reassure me that I'm doing SOMETHING disciplinary.

But still they leap, bark and sail around, ricochet off stools and tables, or collide with one another or me, grabbing at any stray fragment. It may have started when I began cutting up vegetables and tossing cucumber peels, bits of celery, zucchini, etc., on the floor as a neat way to save on trash disposal and give the dogs some extra vitamins.

But that path has led to ruin. Now they all feel that ANYTHING on an upper surface rightfully is theirs, and the sooner it gets on the floor, the better. I lose a lot of food. They grab, jump, paw; they get it!

It's a neat trick to prepare a tricky recipe with a riding crop under one arm, periodically whacking the vertical surfaces or waving it at the slavering horde. But if the whip is dropped, it, too, will be treated as food and instantly chomped. Leather is tasty.

So I've devised ways. I hang the loop on one wrist, and sometimes, as the crop swings around wildly, it knocks over the flour or the milk or the garlic powder. It must be clutched firmly in hand to work right. Some recipes require more rigorous use of the crop, like the traditional turkey dinner, which drives dogs into unparalleled frenzy. Here we may actually have to flick a nose or two as the stuffed bird is grabbed by its protruding leg ...

Putting together a chocolate cake really requires TWO crops, as the doggy enthusiasm mounts. You can use a cake mixer and, at the same time, whirl your whip around in time to music, pretending to be a baton twirler at a football game. Sometimes one of the bolder cats enters the scene and goes for the end of the crop ... cats love to bat at things like that ... so you have to be careful not to whack the cat by mistake into (a) the cake mix or (b) the ten-dog melee.

When things eventually get cooked and put together, it all has to get to the dining table (intact), where the dogs are not allowed (often). Passing through the door with a platter requires BOTH hands, and this is really when you NEED the whip and haven't a third hand. You can use your feet and shove or push dogs back, set down the platter momentarily, lay about with the crop and bang away at all the surfaces. Then try to grab the platter and get through the door. Usually, one very agile and enterprising young dog with criminal tendencies will dash through your legs, beat you into the dining room, to your surprise, in time to make a leap for the platter before you can set it on the table. So all you can do is grab for your whip sticking out of your hip pocket and whack away, upsetting the wine bottle, probably.

This has all been going on here for generations. It didn't happen when I had only one dog. When I had two, there was a hint. Three, and the problem began to manifest. Now, with ten, it is a wolf pack. I have the kind of dogs with appetites that have no discrimination. They'll fight me for a tea bag. So any of my more elegant recipes sets them into a form of canine madness that cannot be dealt with short of whips. But they are all wise to me since THEY don't get whacked. The whips wear out rapidly due to hard life, so it's back to the tack shop, where perhaps they think I am a rabid rider of wild stallions, and they ought to call the humane society.

Days of Our Lives

Data Processing and Clutter

What makes an over-dogged and harried life more interesting are the little things that crop up almost daily, pointing up what a curious and unique life we doggers lead. Recently a phone call came in, of course, JUST as I was cooking up a nourishing and noxious mess for the dogs which was about to burn down. (It did.) I answered it in the usual flustered manner, shoving aside several puppies who were chewing on the phone cord again, and heard a suave, cultured voice asking if this was Carry-On. I immediately envisioned the caller – a gorgeous young woman, smart sophisticated, beautifully dressed (unlike me), the smart executive type. I hated her right off. Then she unbelievably asked, "Can I speak to your data processing manager?" Only a person with a doggy establishment like mine could imagine the shock of this! I shrieked, as I rescued the telephone cord again, "DATA PROCESSING! ARE YOU CRAZY? IN THIS KENNEL?" I hung up.

The whole concept was so amazing, just to imagine ME having such a thing. I have barely mastered the manual typewriter and TV, and I haven't yet moved up to a computer or a VCR ... and a MANAGER! WHO would process MY data? Some years ago the cleaning lady quit, stating that she could no longer battle dog hairs and magazines. My "data" is processed by ME with a little help from the multiple dogs and cats who regularly scatter it about, tear it up, throw up on it, or worse. I file most things in sky-high piles on the dining table or the typing table, at such altitudes that inevitably it all topples over. But things HAVE to be readily at hand. There's NO way that papers and letters can be put away in drawers, etc. I've tried that system in the past, and items I carefully stashed away neatly stayed there for years, forgotten; and those I did search for eventually became outdated. No, everything must be at hand, all those dated premium lists and bills and vet reports and notices of sem-

inars. Also there must be reminder notes and lists in all sorts of strategic places, pinned here and there to remind me to get pills, stool samples or dog food. Things must be handy!

Of course, this piling up process means that to locate even one small item one must go through masses of papers, but even that has its benefit. You KNOW that the article you tore out on some new disease will be at the very bottom of several piles on the south side of the big dining table, or else on the north side of the typing table, so you have to get at it. In the process of sifting it all through, it's likely you again run across numerous other things you tried vainly to find last week; so now you become immersed in those, plus other interesting items which must be studied. This all takes time, while the puppies are unwatched and chew the phone cord again. (I've had an average of three new phones a litter ...)

It's not enough to have the usual dog breeder's clutter, but add to that the things that make up an artist's life. I have twelve rooms, a garage, and a workshop of more material than would fill a warehouse! All of it is precious to me ... to an outsider, it's just junk! But a vast majority of it is fascinating to dogs and cats. One room houses a million pastel sticks, all expensive. The cats love to roll them onto the floor, then they forget them; so the dogs come along and crunch on them, drop them on the floor. Then my treading foot will find them later and grind them into the carpet, especially the darker sticks which leave lifelong spots.

Bags of clay are objects that the dogs love to dig into, and, of course, this makes holes in the plastic so the clay is exposed and dries up if I don't catch it in time. Nothing is more fun to chew on than expensive and hard to find modeling tools. Some that I've had for fifty years are part of my soul! Plaster molds are fun to chew on, too, and provide entertainment, like bones, so here again one must watch. Any studio is full of the weirdest assortment of tools and objects, all of which are fair game for young dogs who will try their teeth on anything handy, perhaps drag it into their crates; I'll find it later, a ruin. I am convinced there is nothing whatsoever that is safe from my horde. They are enterprising enough to try anything, not once, but over and over, despite my frantic yells and chastisement. Spoons, for instance, make good chewing and come out all crumpled, even the old family sterling. Balls of string afford endless fun. The less said about socks and pantyhose the better ... no place is safe for THEM. Books and magazines, of which I have a zillion, give hours of quiet enjoyment to the literary-minded dog when there is nothing better than a quiet gnaw on a pile in the living room.

Not everyone seems to have this problem. Puppies that go from here to their new homes seem to undergo a transformation, so that lets me know that it's all MY fault – the permissive owner who hasn't got her act together. Puppies placed in new homes have extensive toy boxes, I'm told, and even learn to put their toys back in the box (they have data processing managers), and they are ALL housebroken in a week, sleep in the owner's beds, ask to go out, and never steal from the cat. I never experience any of this. I tell myself it's the pack syndrome here, like at an elementary school where even the best child becomes a member of an unruly gang when in a group. Each one hones up its wits to outdo the others in innovative mischief. And, of course, this is likely because all my dogs are so BRILLIANT! They have exceptional minds from dog-school training so are not content with a simple toy or a bed ... no, they must have challenging projects, like some exceptional children must have Nintendos and Lego toys and even chess games. Some of this brilliance may be temporarily lost in the ring, but it's there, lurking, and will invariably come to the fore, especially when new objects come into the house from a shopping trip ... beware the grocery bags ... that way leads to madness!

Most of the people who come into my house are ones I've retrained through the years for their understanding of an off-beat establishment; but, of course, few of them are QUITE so doggy as I am, and their houses have never sunk so low. One comment I'm always hearing, for what it's worth may be, is "Oh! You have such an INTERESTING house! I never come here without seeing something I didn't notice before!" This I usually — and hopefully — take to mean they have spied a new dog figurine on the cluttered mantle that they hadn't seen before, or a new print or maybe my latest art effort. But there are times I strongly suspect they have other meanings. Someone has spied an article of underwear behind a chair where a dog was working on it unbeknownst to me. Or a decapitated field mouse that a cat has abandoned, and a dog has further worked on, was left in a prominent spot. Or an empty dog food can resides on the best chair. Or an old bone all covered in ants has been discovered Or an unmentionable mistake from a puppy that I hadn't noticed, but which a guest always walks through, is found. Or they see the unbelievable rat's nest some industrious dog has made of the couch cover or one of the cushions with the stuffing all out. No amount of vigilance will alter this long and varied list or ever prepare the place for the casual guest. Just weed out all persons except those with worse dogs, and you may get by.

Carpet Cleaning

Having lived so long in an over-dogged household, I'm sure there will never be anything new happening to surprise me, just a repeat of old episodes. I'm wrong. There's ALWAYS something new and traumatic just around the corner. Today it was the rug cleaners. Not that it's a new occurrence as they come every year in a sort of pointless effort to slow down the puddle spots and evidence of zoo life.

I'm pretty well-versed in the whole project ... vacuum thoroughly, remove old bones, toys, balls, hair fuzzies, and some of the lighter furniture. Incarcerate all dogs in their crates and shut all cats in bedrooms. What can go wrong?

But it's always a different ball game. And each year, in an effort to get more efficiency from the process, I try a different rug firm. Each year a new man comes, and even having been warned on the phone beforehand that I "have dogs," he is momentarily spellbound. Beanbags are piled on top of massive chairs, dog baskets and cat condominiums are piled on top of unmovable coffee tables that are unmovable because they have such heavy piles of *Gazettes*, etc. I cheerily tell the man that the deal is to do the "traffic areas" and don't worry about moving the big things. (They haven't been moved in MY lifetime and presumably won't be.) And to do a little extra with the deodorant on the couch area because one of the worst cats I've ever had has had his way with it.

Then I carefully read labels on all the solutions he is to use and ask a lot of questions about how long before it's safe to let the animals walk on the area. So, thus reassured that after a suitable period with all windows and doors open and a fan, all will be well, I let him get busy ... which means a roaring machine, a lethal looking tank spray, and miles of a hose that snakes out the door through the yard and garden flattening flowers.

About that time the traffic starts ... I remember I have to get upstairs to the whelping room with mama dog's dish of goodies and check on the newborns. Then I must carry HER down to visit the lawn, stepping over a tangled octopus of hose and braving the chaos. One of the cats escapes and is horrified at the business going on and has to be chased, cornered and rescued from on top of the trophy shelves, amid crashing Royal Doulton dogs and such.

The crated members in the basement are aware of something very unusual going on and are barking deafeningly; so they need to be soothed and taken out back in the dog yard. From there they can easily SEE the rug cleaner truck and hear its roar, and that sets them off again.

The dining room is also to be done, and there it's hopeless to even contemplate moving the vast massive oak dining table. Piled on top are stacks of pedigrees, premium lists and much else that was hastily gathered from other surfaces, now displaced. Several dogs in the kitchen are only too aware of all the doings and can almost see through the opening we call the "dumb waiter" where food is passed through. More howls of protest. About that time I have to get through to the kitchen for something, letting out one or two frantic members, (I'm not as quick as I was ...) and they are SURE that rug man is a creature from outer space who must be challenged and overcome, to say nothing of his infernal machine and all that smelly spray. As it's probably toxic, I am screaming unheard commands as I round them all up!

Finally it's all done, surprisingly efficiently I must say. The man departs, leaving me with a leftover gallon of his special magic super whooper deluxe space-age deodorant which he privately knows I'll be needing soon.

I set a tall fan in place and open all the windows and doors letting in more moths than I can handle and settle down to watch the rugs dry and renew their youth. But it isn't long before the upstairs mama dog has to come down, cats are yowling to get out, and none can be trusted with an open door.

Gradually life will return to normal, meaning traffic areas will soon be trafficked upon heavily.

I'm herding each dog in and out beady-eyed with watchfulness, especially the VERY old dogs who can't see well and don't give a hoot anyway and are all too famous for spending their puddles most anywhere enroute in or out.

The first one that makes so much as a DROP of puddle here will be sent to the local animal shelter, I swear, knowing I don't mean it. Gradually I survey muddy pawprints from someone who has knocked over the birdbath and then tramped through the dirt. Some grass stains ... an old bone ... a fluff of dog hair ... the two white cats have had a rough and tumble and torn out more hair ... things are not quite as they were when the rug man left. I try to walk through with giant steps, but dogs go leisurely, stopping to scratch on a wet rug probably soaking up who knows what toxic material. I worry.

The weather is humid, and this drying process will go on for days; the bean bags can't go back; the coffee tables with the piles of *Gazettes* are making marks on the rug pile ... nothing can be restored to old times. The fan must roar for days, and I dread a cat's tail getting caught in it. But the old historical mildew stains from long-past puddles seem to be gone! A miracle of the modern age! I know it's only temporary, but how great it is!

I know other people in non-doggy houses who get their Oriental rugs cleaned at vast expense, sending them away for loving care; and while they're

the Culprit....

gone, they have the floor boards redone, sanded, etc. No "traffic area only" cleaning for them. They just move out and go on a cruise while it's being done. I'm lucky the rug man doesn't take one look and back off. In a few days ... or so ... everything will be back to normal, "the way we were" as the song goes. A few sneaky puddles will appear, new puppies will start autographing places, the couch will get it from the bad cat, and there will be bone stains here and there. Meanwhile I'll schedule my overdue dinner party plans for this brief period when my house is almost like other people's homes!

Goodbye, Old Couch

Over the years, I've written so many heartfelt eulogies for my devoted dogs with tears in my eyes and a sad heart, and I will probably go on doing so as the dog population never seems to lessen. But now I will write a few parting words, some of merit and some of great relief, at the final good-bye to my old veteran couch. It is going to its final rest at the landfill dump, and not a moment too soon! I shall miss its massive old bulk but not its odors of 73 years, which is its age.

Somehow, it has had a rather hard life and perhaps not too happy. Handsome in its youth, it was the gem of its day, about 1920. When it looked a bit worn, it was decked out with slipcovers through the years. My father had his final stroke on this couch, but we didn't blame it. But when the dog years began in earnest, the couch was, of course, a favorite spot ... and spots it acquired!

My very first litter was born on that couch ... me being so ignorant I had no proper whelping pen or calendar! My mother supervised ... I hid in the next room and anxiously queried, "Another one! What color?" to which my mother replied happily, "A darling little black one with a white shirt front!" That wasn't the last litter! Many generations have enjoyed the couch and had great good times from puppyhood to old age, all adding to the couch's ruin. It's always been a favorite spot to retire, all alone, and throw up. And it's a favorite spot to camp on with a big greasy bone, freshly dug up and maybe covered with ants. It's a favorite spot to hide old gnawed objects, digging deeply through the current slipcover into the stuffing.

Dear Cream Tea, who in fifteen years never put a foot wrong, once stepped out of character and chewed a great hole through the back. After my initial frenzy, I managed to crisscross it with duct tape and get yet another slipcover.

Several new young dogs, left alone and unobserved, chewed the arms down to the wood frame, letting me have a chance to observe how well furniture was put together in the 1920's!

Then there were the cats. I've had cats, in threes, since age seven, with few problems; but the current batch have had strange interactions and behaviors no cat breeder can explain. All altered and amicable, they began to "mark" territory, always unobserved. But nothing ... I repeat, nothing ... is as persistent as cat pee. So began a long list of remedies, more surefire pet deodorants than I can count, even ones no one would believe; like expensive sprays smelling like bubble gum which are used by morticians. Nothing worked. But the dogs didn't mind and kept rummaging about, hiding objects and chewing. One exception was the day I set a large rat trap to scare the cats; a dog set it off and catapulted across the room in terror.

I have recently suspected there were mice deep in the back stuffing, as the cats lurk about and have caught some. Mice are clever, and I admire them a lot. They tend to raid the dog-food bucket at night and carry off pellets by the dozen to amass a store for a later feast, perhaps in a boot or a duffel bag or the couch back. The couch is so constructed that there is no room at all under it for a vacuum or a broom. What happens to go under it stays – unless I have lost a valuable and get down on my stomach and poke with a rod. Out may come several small balls, a rubber mouse, old Christmas ornaments, and an old bone.

For years elderly dogs have cozied up, head on one arm, drooling and scratching luxuriously. One knows how the wind blows when they can no longer manage to jump up. The summer heat and humidity this season are bringing out all the scents of past years on the old veteran. It's no longer to be tolerated. The days of carpet powder, Clorox, and sprays are over. Why haven't I bid it good-bye long since? No one would move it! They don't make 'em that massive now. No one had a truck with the $25 dump sticker ... up to now. But at last it is solved ... I found a stalwart neighbor who says he can do it; he has a truck, so it's finally the time to part! I'm hoping the kids of the neighborhood and the various neat housewives won't congregate about as the old whale gets loaded; men will be groaning, and dogs will be barking and keening as the old familiar "pet odors" (polite term) waft about the area. I'd like it to be taken out in the dead of night, duct tape shining, shedding a last bit of stuffing, dogs howling good-bye. I shall not go to the dump with it but just say good-bye and thanks for the seventy-odd years of service, while I plan my next move, a search for something smaller and possibly with far less upholstery.

Actually, there IS no ideal couch. I've been through the bean bags, love seats, settees, vinyl, and nothing is foolproof with a gang of dogs. But starting fresh, with a liberal dose of dog and cat repellent, I might get by for a while.

My latest plan is to get periodical smaller replacements at the local Salvation Army store and rotate them. Off to the dump with it, and then get another; so on and on till the dog population peters out, or I do. Only prob-

...in my old age I eat my meagre meals out of my vast store of tarnished show trophies....

lem, as I now put this plan in motion, is that no HUMAN can use the couch or even that end of the room due to the newest most SUPER offensive dog and cat repellent. But the animals haven't seemed to mind it a bit.

Demi-Disasters

Only a doggy household can have hourly, regular demi-disasters. I might be down in the basement struggling with the overgrown coat and mandarin nails of an eight-month-old puppy whose owner has finally condescended to bring it back for repairs. After this debacle, wherein the victim has knocked over sundry cans of spray, shears and clippers that clattered to the floor on the hard cement ... you go upstairs. Voila! ... You emerge into the kitchen into a dense London fog of smoke ... no, the house is not on fire ... yet, ... but I had forgotten that a couple of pounds of liver was merrily boiling away on the stove, being readied for training and tracking practice. Alas, now it is no more than a fossilized cinder, and my best pot is encrusted with black crud.

Doors and windows must all be thrown wide open, and Lysol and Nilodor are lavishly sprayed. As smoke rises, the bedrooms are also hazy with the stuff. Over all hangs a miasmic pall of burned liver, not to be dispelled for many a day. Guests will come by and remark for weeks ... "Oh, you're cooking something?"

But one such event is never enough in any given dog day. Off to training class in early evening and a last look around, as the mind grows cunning and sly in an attempt to outthink, out-wit and out-anticipate the furry ones. Cats are accounted for, and Old Dog is shut in the kitchen. Newspapers are laid down. Everything is checked.

Upon the midnight return, it appears that Old Dog in the kitchen had company. Fat Dog was ALSO hidden away in the depths of the puppy cage, as was Siamese who escaped into the kitchen via the dumb waiter passageway which is through the china cabinet ... smashing several heirloom glass objects.

Fat Dog must really have been frustrated with so little to steal, but as usual, as ALWAYS, came off a winner. This time it was a quart can of maple syrup. She easily opened the top, which is something I can hardly ever do myself short of banging, hammering and hot water. Maple syrup was wall to wall on the linoleum; newspapers were stuck in it; and Fat Dog had, by my estimate, consumed the better part of the quart. Incredible! But there's more ...

The gallon water dispenser was empty and knocked over. Fat Dog was frantic! She then drank a quart of water before she was forcibly stopped, and her figure resembled a hippo's. Anyone can guess the rest. Crated Fat Dog whimpered half the night, not with a tummy ache, as no food existing could ever render that iron-clad stomach into discomfort, but the water consumption had the expected effect. Several trips to the yard were made in the dead of night.

This of course wakes a person up after a while, so it seemed a good time to inspect my trap lines. (Another story here ...) For some time I have been troubled with mice (large ones) or rats (small ones) — take your choice, but Purina fans all. When I discovered a young one emerging up from a dog dish where I had scooped Purina into Alpo and milk, whiskers dripping, and Alpo on his head, I knew it was time for me to be the exterminator. (Much as I hate depriving even a bug of its jolly existence.) One by one these rodents met their grisly fate in a large and lethal rat trap. But the victims were never-ending. I set the traps by the Purina bag and got to snaring one or two every night. The disposal of the furry corpses always brought problems as ALL canines and felines had to get into the act.

They come from everywhere once I have a departed rodent by the tail. Leaping shoulder high, one or another dog has snagged the victim and rushed hysterically off to crate, den, bed, or couch to worry, gnaw, toss, and eventually try to bury it in any good place, under the bed, or a rug, etc. (I'll find out much later.) Or a feline will climb my leg and snatch the corpus delecti from me to go through much the same primitive ritual. EVERYONE is excited over a second-hand mouse, but no one actually seems to eat it. I have often gotten as far as the back porch and flung the hapless creature far into the woods. Out of nowhere springs a cat or dog who dashes after it in the best field-trial retriever fashion and brings it back eventually to the back porch.

On the other hand, rodents NOT second-hand do not fare even as well. Once Omar cat was toying with a chipmunk alive, alive-o. Since this could not be tolerated, I must rush to the rescue; but, as always, the canines outwit me, tumbling out the door first in mad pursuit (me screaming obedience commands that fall on deaf ears). First to reach the scene is, of course, the Avid Eater, who hardly pauses in the mad gallop, swoops and swallows the chipmunk alive, alive-o. What a sick story ... really traumatic. And, of course, Avid Eater had just been divested of ever-present worms from just such game eating.

In an Ann Landers column, I read the results of a survey. Seventy percent of the people polled said if they had to do it all over, they wouldn't have children. Some elderlies said that their children didn't care about all they had done for them. Others said that they had been happy, well-adjusted career people until they had children and were now screaming, nagging, nervous wrecks. Well, I'm in much the same boat, and I even PLANNED my canine children. Not one will give a hoot when I'm old and feeble if I'm not on time with each dinner bowl, being too arthritic to open a can or bend down. They'll doubtless knock me down and open the cans with their teeth ... and then leave for a better neighborhood!

As for my pre-dog days, though, I can hardly cast my memory back to that unfamiliar era. Yes, I, too, was a well-adjusted career person, and had many other attributes – neat, clean, unhairy as to clothes, unhampered, unfettered as to social life, quiet, leisurely, calm, introspective, creative ... I could go on. Now I, too, am a screaming, nagging wreck, vainly trying to take up the slack of years and conscious of the losing fight against small insidious backsliding.

A very few dog-club friends seem to keep a house full of animals and appear neat, serene and capable. More of us, however, are like me, always a bit hairy, a trifle unkempt, house less than *Better Homes and Gardens*, piles of *Gazettes* cascading off the hassocks and end tables, and trophies slightly tarnished everywhere. Chew-sticks and bones are in chairs and squeakies are underfoot. Knotted socks lie here and there. A bit of chewed furniture is apparent, too!

The answer lies in total crating and kenneling, but what hard-heart would not allow "just a few house individuals"? And what about these puppies who MUST be socialized, although the rug has had years of all the current spot remedies? Not for nothing do close friends call this "Pine-Sol Acres." You know you've had it when your best friends send you 25 cents-off coupons on the giant 40-oz. size of Pine-Sol!

Random Thoughts

How do I love thee? Let me count the ways ... (the poet says). So say I as I survey the trash basket overturned, its contents in all corners of the kitchen. I only left the room for five minutes. WHY do I love them? They haven't a redeeming quality, the rotten things. Someone peers out from the dog bed, cat food can in mouth, doing the reconnaissance bit to see if I am militant or, as usual, hopelessly resigned. I have been through a long variety of trash baskets graduating from simple to complex with a trap door cover, then to a fancy Mexican wicker one. None are dog proof. The last receptacle now resides permanently on a counter top, inconvenient and unconventional, but reasonably safe.

Shopping night is always hairy. One returns laden with multiple bundles, and if foolish enough to set them down for even a minute to open a gate or a door, the horde is into them with great expertise, picking out the choice things. Naturally the bag of dog bones is first to be detected, but not immune are the green peppers, a great favorite. These are snatched and dashed off with to be devoured with great haste on the couch. Later pepper seeds are found scattered for a mile all over the rug. If one is not really vigilant, other commodities are removed and sampled. Soap is often removed from the wrapper and tooth marked. Toilet paper is worth a brief interest, just enough to shred the roll irrevocably. Other edible oddments are removed from bags and spirited off to dog beds for later sampling, and it's a dark day when the packages of rice and macaroni are opened and contents strewn about in inaccessible places. All this occurs when one is not in charge and leaves a shopping bag unattended for even a short time. Inedible things come in for attention when all else fails, so that one finds packages of pantyhose, inner soles, or similar soft goods in the process of destruction in one of the dog beds.

Then comes the glorious moment when the dog bones are dispensed, and it is a scramble to get each individual to her crate before the bone is removed to a chair or couch, which is after all the BEST place to gnaw.

Nothing ever improves here dogwise. One by one, annoyances are just borne with increasing fortitude until they become almost bearable. Finally one hardly notices the sins of the canines until one is jarred into reality by some guest who is aghast at some of the things that occur and says so ... this is a commentary on how far we have slipped into tolerances of our fur people.

After many years of total dog negativism, my next door neighbors have acquired a dog for no discernible reason except it was a gift. I am watching their rapid dissolution into the sub-culture. I fully expect to witness the ultimate step on the downward path of dedication as I see, some night, out dog walking, equipped with flashlight, baggie and box, my neighbor standing ready to snare the stool sample for the morning vet trip. Many other things follow suit. They become hooked on dog obedience classes, then breed handling, then a tentative trip to a local match. This sets the tone; next is a show, complete with vast picnic cooler. When the disease finally sets in, the sub-culture has another victim making out entries, planning trips, thinking about the circuits, motels, and good times.

The garden season is on, with its hazards. In May, little seedlings and transplants, though protected by low fences, are at the mercy of the four foot-

The Carry-Ons share everything — but there are times when one does not want to share Rubber Ducky and other treasures....

ed ones, who gaily trample through the beds in search of toads, mice or whatever. As the season advances, the plants become larger, but more brittle, and do not recover so well from the tromping paw. Then in midsummer, the high bushy perennials take a beating from canine safaris into their depths. Just what is to be discovered in the plant beds escapes me, but it is a constant source of fascination. With dogs you stand rather little chance of having *Better Homes and Gardens* visit you for a feature on your horticultural wonders. I have never yet found the solution for dead spots on lawns from puddles.

I am growing a new variety of patio tomato in a vast pot, and everyone seems to have her eye on them. What doesn't get broken off will probably be eaten upon ripening.

I am working on a good answer for the people who ask gently if I am perhaps not getting too doggy. All things in moderation, they murmur kindly. I am farther away from the answer all the time.

I am beginning to wonder myself sometimes ...

In the Future

Some day, after my several hundreth litter, and the ever renewed acute anguish of seeing old dogs through their last days, I may make the ultimate mistake and decide to keep several promising youngsters out of a litter when I had SWORN I would breed no more, would limit the population, and gradually phase out of dogs in view of my advancing years.

I'm sure there will be canine comments as I totter about, like OldDog, trying to keep up the facade of vigorous health. One puppy will remark to a teenage dog: "Well, she looks more shaky than usual today. That's the second pan of dog food she's dropped on her shoe. Lucky we're here to clean up!"

"Yes, and last night WE got the corned beef hash and SHE fried the ALPO. It's things like that which make me wonder about her nowadays."

"Well, grandma always told us there had been signs some time back. Of course, she was ALWAYS eccentric, but nowdays I often wonder where she'll end up. Like she can't hear us bark to get out ever since we chewed up her hearing aid."

"Not that I'd be the first to be disloyal, but it makes me wonder about the future. I might pack my squeaky toys and set off for that Animal Shelter place where all the movie stars sponsor the dogs. I'd be sure to be adopted into a super home."

"Yes, I see what you mean. I never really did dig the motivation in back of that Greyfriar's Bobby yarn. It's all very well to go to your master's grave and have a statue raised to you in Scotland; but I'm practical, and I like a steady supply of groceries."

"Well, there she is putting the leash on that fat old Siamese cat, thinking it's one of us. You shouldn't have chewed up her trifocals."

"Yes, it's sad. Maybe we ought to consider putting her to sleep before it gets any worse."

"But I'd sort of miss her, you know. She has such interesting food slops down the front of her shirt. And she's so slow I can always get to the best shelf in the fridge before she even knows I'm there!"

"Grandma says she used to be very active in the dog shows and tracking and all that stuff. Thank heavens we didn't get in on that era of regimentation! I like to do my own thing, and life here and now IS pretty loose."

"Yes, we'd better not split just yet, man. Maybe they'd stick us in that obedience school if we went elsewhere, and I've heard THAT'S a drag."

"Good thinking ... hey! She fell asleep in her chair. Now we can slurp up her soup."

"Yes, but watch out. She's apt to have it laced with brandy."

"Well, at her age, what's left?"

III.
The Breeding Game

One of my less desirable neighbors' mongrel dog has just had her umpteenth litter under the back shed, sans post-pit shot, worming, or other medical attention, but thriving on dubious fare, when and if; and her brood has achieved robust development without a care in the world. Wouldn't you know ... Here sit I, deep in my pharmacy of nostrums from vet and kennel supplier, with a path worn smooth to the vet's door. Nothing for MY puppies is left undone from birth until they leave for their new homes.

Worming usually goes smoothly, but the occasional bout of gastro-intestinal diarrhea is a gas, to coin a phrase. Three pills per pup thrice daily times nine pups, plus boiled rice thrice daily times nine stools thrice daily ... I've lost count ... adds up to innumerable trash bags of used newspapers and endless times on the haunches picking them up and laying them down ... plus cleaning up the little ones and picking rice grains out of their fur.

I think it's safer, however, to have dogs than children. When faced with the various intolerable irritations, one can shriek invectives at the dogs without fear of wounding their delicate psyches and having them whine to their psychiatrists at a later age. Shriek away; dogs rarely take it to heart for long!

After the hundredth litter, I just know I will be nominated for membership in the Mensa Club, that organization that takes only people with enormous IQs. I am constantly amassing information and culture. I may SEEM to read the Sunday papers, but it is only cursory. Not until I am in the puppy pen amid scratching and biting individuals do I manage to get my real culture. My eye catches a certain fascinating item amid the multiple doo-doos, and I am mesmerized as I try to read it, in a frog-like position with puppies all over me, shredding the garments. It is invariably a meaty piece of information that I previously overlooked, such as the statistics on hermaphroditic frogs in Yugoslavia or what the stock market statistics are on soy bean facial packs. Or it may be some very intellectual article on the Avant Garde theater off Broadway that I really must know about. Whatever it is, I had missed it when reading the paper in its original form. Somehow, covered with puppy stuff, it seems to be enhanced and offers up to me hitherto undreamt-of bits of learning my soul cannot do without. I even tear out items of interest to save!

All this leads to a longer time in the puppy pen than planned for and also leads to runs in the stockings if one is silly enough to wear them, or frayed slacks, chewed shoes and other depredations. Finally one is laden with the lawn and garden bags filled up with newspapers on the way to the trash department. Barring a cremation, it is a problem and many a trash man grumbles.

So you place ads in all the papers after your show types have gone, and ruin your bank balance as you go all out to hit all the papers in several adjoining states. Then settle back on a Sunday for the inquiries. They come, and the phone is ringing with all those dingalings who ask, "WHAT is an English Cocker? Is it like a water spaniel?" (What IS a water spaniel? I ask myself.) After some explanation, the caller says thank you and they think they'll get a Dalmatian. Sometimes you make an appointment and give endless directions as to how to find you, the various routes, the back roads, the railroad tracks and the stockade fence – and then they don't show up. Possibly later they will call and whine that they ended up in another state.

How about all those hours when you are endlessly grabbing the boy pups and feeling for testicles and praying. Asking all your breeder friends with agile fingers to come in and have a feel. At last they are there, more welcome than an oasis in the desert after a long safari. Then you check bites for days and days and try to recall other litters which straightened out after they had initially looked like teenagers before a trip to the orthodontist. Then there was the day that the number four pup got his eye cut on a bramble and was rushed to the vet. All was well, but "come back three days later." At that appointed time, you grabbed the pup from the squiggling mass and were on your way to the vet's, twenty miles distant, and discovered in the waiting room that you had grabbed the wrong puppy and had a girl instead of a boy ... and the receptionist gently told you that there WAS a way to tell the difference.

How many times in the night have you leaped out of bed, hearing a mad wail and a horrible yelping, thinking of some dire thing, only to be greeted with six or more little faces and patty paws at the gate, awaiting attention with absolutely nothing wrong?

Is it worth it, you ask? Then there

comes a letter in the mail telling you that dear little Cornelius has settled into his new home, is enrolled in obedience class, and is the darling of the household, and will be back for a trim next month before his first match. Enclosed is a blurred Polaroid snapshot of little Cornelius, looking darling; and you are overcome with grandmotherly affection. Feeling like the Old Woman in the Shoe with multiple progeny, you quietly plan your next breeding ... the vet meanwhile rubs his hands in anticipation of your entire bank roll.

Sex and the Single Dog

Sooner or later this subject WILL rear its head in most doggy establishments. Even the one-pet-owner has to cope with it eventually before deciding on some measures to take. (Like the slogan, "neuter is neater.") During breeding season here at Carry-On, the girls act like nymphomaniacs, making up to the cats, which goes over like a lead balloon since the cats are all altered males and still bitter about it. But as the zero hour of whelping approaches, all the girls roll their limpid eyes at me in misery, mutely saying, "WHY did I fall? It wasn't worth it ... never again ... gimme the pill."

Even old grandma, after many litters, arrives in season eternally young and full of zap, flirting her tail at the boy dog and inviting him out behind the barn, never recalling all those dreary days feeding and cleaning up after the pups when she looked as if she would expire of boredom.

But of course the FIRST days of her kids were fun, when mama raged at the male with a passion, as if to say, "YOU did this to me, you monster, but now they're MINE, so bug off! I'm bringing them up MY way!"

The attitude of the male all through the season is that of eternal hope. Shut in the basement in cloistered seclusion, he never gives up, never ceases whining and bellowing, never misses a chance to make a hopeful pass at the cat, and cheerily waters down all vertical surfaces.

Little does old matron dog seem to realize, as she cavorts about, that she will spend many dreary hours dumped down in the depths of the sofa, looking like a fat toad engorged with flies, awaiting the glorious hour of deliverance.

When all the girls in the house are in season, one triggering another so that they are ALWAYS in together, but staggered – first one, then another a week later and so on until the whole episode takes about seven weeks – then frustrations abound. With the only available real gent incarcerated down in the kennel, one must make do with whatever is around for fun and games. This ranges from each other to the cats. Poor substitutes, but any port in a storm and there are some weird pseudo-copulations at the in-season time. Always trying, to say the least, especially when one is faced with a visit from some church-oriented person or an elderly aunt, viewing such rampant sex with a horrified eye. No shame! No inhibitions! But all in the daily dog game, and everyone, from dogs to cats to people, will forget the whole taboo subject and cluster around cooing and gushing when the puppies arrive!

The Perils of Progesterone Predictions

How well I remember the Dud-Stud party ... that was when friends traveled many a mile for a get-together to consummate an important breeding between two well-matched breeding partners, both rookies! Refreshments were laid in and time allotted for able hands who were to assist at this highly important pairing. Alas, it never got off the launching pad. Both dogs were totally dedicated to celibacy and nothing would induce the least carnal thoughts, let alone deeds.

Sometimes in this present age it seems all there is around us is politics and sleaze. Porn is everywhere. It's nice to be able to retreat into the world of dogs and see only love and purity ... almost. I recall one of my illustrious breedings which I had approached with fasting and prayer, doing all the best nutrition, raspberry leaves, etc. Alerted the vet, the stud's owners, had the progesterone test ... all bases were covered, and then one day she was in season! The troops swung into action on the VERY day she was supposedly the most fertile. But science is often wrong.

In this household of usually ten bitches from young to old, ALL members are aware of the bitch in season; and, of course, SHE is always sure one of THEM might prove to be a suitable partner, judging from some of the pseudo-couplings that always go on. These weird mating dances usually mean my girl is "ready" for the Big Day. So the owners of Daddy Dog arrive. Instantly he is alerted to the situation even as he alights from the van, eager to give his all to the project. But not my girl! Brought into the room, she shows some sort of violent change of opinion about the whole matter and is now a flag bearer for chastity. With screams of protest and outrage, she flies onto a chair and snarls epithets to this rapist. Not yet deterred, he presses on valiantly, only to get a face full of teeth as she flies about from chair to chair and behind people.

This was a real switch from the scene with my other bitches, and I wondered about the vet's progesterone diagnosis. We decided to take it calmly and just persevere. I taped her muzzle which meant that she panted heavily, puffing out her cheeks like a spring peeper frog. Two of us hardy souls held her in a death grip while two more steadied Daddy Dog, who really didn't need much encouragement but WAS getting frustrated.

But it was all a disaster. She threw herself down in a reverse twist out of our grasp, and he was left working on nothing to his chagrin. We righted her and tried again ... and again ... but it got worse as she used ever new and clever contortions to slither out of our grasp.

Finally, after an hour or so, we retired for coffee and let the two ill-assorted subjects go their own way. Pretty soon we saw that things had taken a slightly better turn as she stood with a hint of a flag to her tail! We leaped up, scattering cake and coffee far and wide and were hard at it again, all four of us on the floor, knees protesting, doing our guidance thing. Though perhaps a shade better, it was about the same as before, and it became obvious that there would be no vital connection that day; and besides, the conversation was getting pretty graphic.

One member of the crew had given up, claiming a charley horse and was sitting by the fireplace doubled up laughing at the spectacle of the other three on the floor, heads down on the rug, peering under the dogs and making as decent observations as we could without losing our cool and sinking to porn! But still it didn't work.

We finally gave up, and the dogs retired to different parts of the room and flopped down, dead beat, and went to sleep. We spent a bit more time with coffee and swapped tales along the line of the neighbor's dog let out to piddle who was bred instantly by a passing stranger and had a litter of twelve under the porch. We made a date to resume operations the next day. My girl staggered up with one last scowl at Daddy Dog and went into the kitchen to resume her posturings with the other gang of bitches – all of whom had heard the sounds of the festivities and wanted to know more.

Hopeful – at 6 months   Hopeful – at 18 months

The Breeding Game

the houseful of show prospects that turned out to be house-duds living on to age 16.

Well, the next day Daddy Dog was brought over at 11 a.m., and we all said the polite and hopeful things. I let my girl into the room. She evidently had a night to think it over and perhaps had a long talk with one of the older bitches ... one will never know, but she galloped into the room, barked a happy greeting, and LEAPED on Daddy Dog, knocking him over! He recovered himself and said, "This time for real, kid!" and it was done in a second! No one had to hold anyone. It was just like the tales of the neighbors' dogs! We hardly had time to get down on our knees again and hold the now-tied couple for the next half hour. Talk about progesterone levels ... there must be a fine line from total "No-no!" to "Yes-yes!" My knees weren't the same for weeks.

Puppies

Puppies – Do you really understand what it entails to state that your puppies are "home-raised" or socialized in a true home environment or to make any of those statements implying that they are raised – not coldly in a kennel – but in the bosom of your household? This means, in my case, upheaval from six weeks on. For the first four weeks, all is peace as you watch the wee ones sleeping in a huddle, dependent on mama; and you can't wait to enjoy their puppyhood.

The time comes! On fine days, even in winter, they can go out for supervised romps; but that word "supervised" means old eagle eye goes out also, seeing no one comes to harm! Romps on the lawn to socialize mean extra vigilance, since in every season there are perils – tulips and spring flowers to destroy, summer blooms to nip, holes to be dug in grass, evergreens to chew.

But the real exhaustifier is the socialization on inclement days or days when one is too busy to get to the small fry until late. Then they are let out of the puppy room to romp and get used to life. Sojourns in the kitchen are great, being introduced to the waste basket and the trash, to big scary things that live there. Possibly that's where the lifelong refrigerator syndrome begins! As you move about keeping busy with endless chores, a flock of little ones thunder in pursuit of your feet, causing you to fall, trip, lurch, or even step on one, occasioning blood-curdling yelps. It isn't any good to think you can utilize the socializing hour to do a useful chore such as putting away laundry or something. Disaster follows in rapid succession. Things are knocked over, bumped into, broken or chewed; and, unless you are vigilant, puddles and worse are sneakily and casually left in corners only to be discovered much later ... on a damp day perhaps. Nothing can be left unsurveyed. Shoes are spirited off, as are socks, and anything else left on the floor or a low place. In the case of a fairly large house, one or another of the crew disappears into far rooms, under chairs, gets lost, possibly far under the bed and generally requires a search party. But what a delightful event this socializing is!

The cats, long hardened to bringing up puppy, get in on the act, feigning aloofness and superiority, but secretly delighted to be a part of the scene in which they can usually assert a measure of top-of-the-totem-pole cat-ness. Puppies, in turn, discover the cat and are ecstatic to find that there *is* a live, furry squeaky toy!

This is the time when chores are eventually abandoned while you watch, smile, gurgle, and coo over your darlings; you watch their expressions, traits, personalities, and reactions. Finally, you are on the floor, like a beached whale, with the small fry clambering over you, nibbling ears, and untying shoelaces – and it generally doesn't change much after the 20th litter. THESE are the joys of homeraised puppies!

English Cockers and Cats

English Cockers love cats. They're kindly towards them, unlike some breeds who tend to shred, pounce, swallow, or otherwise demolish cats. English Cockers in England are well known for rabbit hunting, as well as for birds, so some vestigial memory lingers. Perhaps a cat is a surrogate or a substitute rabbit, to be sought after and delivered to hand unharmed.

Cats in the life of an English Cocker have many uses and fill many deep needs. Stealing from the cat's dish is, of course, paramount; although, this usually comes to an end when the owner puts all cat dishes up on high counters. Even so, the average smart EC may find a way, as cat food is so tasty and fishy.

Life is always a matter of balance and contrasts. There are times when I've HAD it with the dogs. Perhaps they have barked hysterically all day at the mailman, UPS, kids and birds, and even imaginary trolls. They've torn my stockings, eaten a plant, broken the pot, dug holes, tracked in mud, made a few "mistakes" in the house, stolen my lunch, gnawed a chair and barked some more. I take some aspirin, make some tea, and shut them in their crates until I reconstruct my wits and soul. It's then that I clutch my elderly Siamese, a truly royal personage, and while he purrs an accompaniment of approbation, I tell him fervently that I'm going into CATS exclusively. No barking, stealing, shedding, hysteria, holes in the lawn, etc., etc. He agrees and feels I am long overdue in reaching this decision.

After a refreshing doze, I wonder where the dogs are ... it's so quiet. Elderly Siamese has fallen asleep, and I realize he doesn't really NEED me; he's so self-sufficient and into Zen Buddhism anyway. So out come the EC's from their crates to bring back the pandemonium afresh ,and gone is my resolution to switch to cats. But then, you gotta have BOTH for balance.

Naturally, a beloved English Cocker must have EVERYTHING in life: toys, people, kids, and possessions galore. Fond owners lavish new squeakies and amusements and pleasures on their loved ones. But the needed ULTIMATE is their very own cat, not always easy to achieve. Due to the inherent independence of most cats, these creatures are often their own man and nobody else's. Nevertheless, this can be remedied by acquiring a new kitten for every new young dog until the right combination is achieved. Try your local Animal Shelter or nearby dairy barn. You'll be helping the cat population explosion and your vet as he spays and neuters your growing army of cats. (Remember that female cats come in season about every half hour unless spayed, despite all vigilance, and have innumerable litters a year ...)

The great trend these days is not necessarily dogs, but CATS, judging from the bookstores where every few days a new cartoon book emerges dealing with cats ... cats on diets, cats alive or dead, cats all over. Therefore, it is fitting to examine the role of cats in the average English Cocker household. Defin-itely they are a MUST. Few other breeds are so fitted for felines. One might even say an English Cocker without his or her own cat lives a half life.

The cat population must include a fine OLD cat, philosophical and bland, wise and kind, who sits up all night by the whelping box and watches the newest batch of EC's into the world. What a marvel it is that this old-timer, death on mice, chipmunks, and squirrels, doesn't attempt to commandeer one of the tiny newborns when mama is out briefly for air. Easily done, they'd surely be tastier than a chipmunk; but this never happens, praise be. A dog is a dog, even at age 20 minutes.

A bit later, this cat will be pressed into service as the four-week olds are brought one at a time to see their first furry toy. Generations of wee puppies have all reacted the same: the groping discovery and the explosion into ecstasy as they realize this is a PERSON IN FUR! Then, always the same, they begin gnawing off the cat's ears! That this is tolerated is another miracle, but many a cat has borne it with patience and only leaves in a huff when things get too much.

So one starts

English Cockers on cats early, and the relationship always reflects joy and love. Even the grumpiest and most withdrawn old Scrooge of a cat seems to instinctively realize that (1) puppies are no great threat, and (2) they are easily beaten up and overpowered if necessary, a feeling that makes any cat feel bigger than life even if the feeling never becomes an established reality.

When the puppies are having romps about the house to socialize, this is when cats best come into play. Only YOUNG cats and kittens enter into active games. Older cats must be treated with respect, so very early the puppies learn from a face full of pins, though it is amazing how cats bat out gently! This is the time, if you have only older cats, that you must really, for the good of your puppy's develop, acquire a KITTEN. (Deprive puppies of nothing lest they grow up neurotic!) So into the house must come a kitten, the wee-er the better. Now the puppies and you won't have to throw the froggie all the time, and you can sit back and howl at the antics of kitten and pups. Or if your litter is too large, get two kittens! Someone will bless you for taking the kittens off their hands.

One of the constant "outs" of ANY cat is the grim fact that English Cockers, who have developed weird gourmet tastes over the centuries, WILL raid cat litterboxes. So buy only the green alfalfa kitty litter ... Face it ... EC's EAT cat-doo spiked with kitty litter and the sharper litter is bad for tummies. There seems no perfect solution for this vice. Some litterboxes are closed with a port hole door. Try that, though most dogs can get their heads in. This is a problem for some clever workshop-type man to solve. Invent a cure, patent it, and get rich.

As you sell each puppy, try to ascertain if the household has a cat, active, young and tolerant. INSIST on it! Your special puppy must not start out with a lack in his life! This is the time to visit the Animal Shelter or dairy barn again; scoop up some more kittens so you can give a free bonus kitten with each puppy. If you are selling that SPECIAL super show puppy, you may want to insist he have, at the least, a Siamese or Persian!

In your home, provide a wicker dog basket, especially in winter, in front of the stove or fireplace. Watch cats and dogs all pile in at once, knitted together, hot as pistols in front of the fire. Run for your camera to take those prize-winning color shots that may win you a trip abroad or one of the 100 lesser (and useless) premiums.

When Old Dog has been relegated to the status of Bed Dog, lying all night on your feet until the circulation stops, then you will notice Old Cat joining you, sometimes curled into Old Dog's feathers or even lapping solicitously the top of her head where Old Cat has discovered a papilloma wart that needs healing. Old Dog and Old Cat have been through the mill, seen nearly two dozen litters into the world, and have earned their retirement, while Next Dog and Next Cat take over the fun and games.

If you don't happen to be a "cat person," so much the worse for you ... and your English Cockers! Think what you all miss! People who hate cats, I've heard, were rats in their last incarnation and harbor a secret subconscious wish to be some predatory breed in their next life and eat cats. Work on your souls, people, and weave cats into your life, and your English Cockers' lives will be enriched!

P.S. This has nothing to do with cats, but a funny overheard at a restaurant recently with (who else) dog people: When asked what she was going to order, the lady replied, "I haven't looked at the premium list yet."

Puppy's New Home

"Tis easy to sell a puppy to someone who has been in contact with you for ages and ages, probably way back when the breeding was merely a thought. Letters have been flitting back and forth and by the time the little one leaves you, you know everything there is to know about the new owner. You've even become privy to some of the intimate details unknown by other family members, the family physician and clergyman. In any case, a puppy buyer who is this much of a confidante is probably already in" dogs." So, being a member of your own charmed circle of those needing no instructions of feeding, care and the rest of the vast body of knowledge encompassing the raising up of even one dog, you can react a little easier over the transition.

But when an inquiry for a puppy comes from a total stranger, the whole transaction takes on a different face. Perhaps this baby is the last grape on the vine and the one no one seemed to want. He may have only one descended testicle; his bite or dentition is still dubious. This pup may be the unlucky bearer of unattractive color or markings, or he may be too big or too small, or fall short of Best in Show potential in some obvious or elusive way. What, then, do we do about placing this not-quite-winner, but DEAREST of all the puppies in the RIGHT home?

As the inquiries come in, WE SCREEN! This must be done more thoroughly than choosing a new President of the United States or a delegate to the United Nations. More pains are taken in ascertaining the suitability of a new home for puppy than in finding a new tax accountant or approving your potential future son-in-law.

No stone must go unturned to ascertain that THIS is the right home and THESE the right people for little Murgatroyd. The first thing to find out is the make of the car they have. If it's any kind of mini or subcompact, foreign or domestic, into which a crate would not comfortably fit, forget the whole thing and terminate the interview right there. Hang up the phone if you have to. If the car

is okay, explain the need for a crate in minute, emphatic detail including makes and sizes. Find out if there is a reputable groomer and pet supplies dealer in their immediate area, and tell them all the items they are going to have to buy if you sell them your treasured pet.

At least a half-hour dissertation on grooming is MANDATORY. Murgatroyd must never be allowed to look like a mop, and it will be the new owner's unwavering duty to see that this is realized. Be sure to get a complete run-down on all immediate neighbors — at least three families on either side. Essential information in this department includes exhaustive dossiers on all neighbor children and any pets that are likely to come into contact with Murgatroyd. And be sure to inquire as to the character and disposition of the newsboy, as this is very vital.

So far, so good. If the prospect does not own a bean bag chair, make him promise to buy one before taking delivery on the puppy. While on the subject of furniture, make sure there are no Early American high beds, like four posters, unless they are equipped with footstools so "Murg" can alight and depart at will without risk of spraining something.

Now there are only a few more really important items to determine about the prospect. What college did the local vet graduate from and what is his specialty? Insist that no one in the house is a jogger, so that the puppy will not exhaust himself following along. No one must be a junk food faddist, either. And be sure they do not own any continuous filament rugs that unravel and pull out teeth when chewed upon!

Extract a solemn promise that all thorn-bearing shrubbery will be permanently removed; and, if there is a swimming pool on the property, the prospect must be ready to erect a 12-foot high stockade fence as an additional safety measure for your baby.

Earlier you found out about the neighbor children. Now it's time to learn about the offspring of the potential buyer. Dwell at length on his or her youngster's temperament, IQ and any behavioral anomalies. But go carefully on the last as this could easily result in the phone being hung up in YOUR ear. Incidentally, while checking out the junior set, look into any potential hazards from elderly relatives with canes, poor eyesight, or uncertain footing.

Ask the location of the electric meter as the meter reader might be an undesirable, and find out about other delivery people that call regularly at what might be Murgatroyd's new digs. Does the nearest obedience school have a high accreditation level without too many dropouts, and will the puppy meet a good class of dogs there?

If you still have the caller's attention at this point, invite the family to come for a tentative look. This is really so you can size them up further in person. At this point, if in any way you don't like the cut of their jib — KEEP THE PUPPY!

IV.
Dog Shows
The Joys of the Shows

A whole new world opens up when the dog fancier finally graduates from handling classes, training classes and matches, and takes the step into the BIG TIME. Premium lists and the *Gazette* are closely scrutinized and advice is given as to the merits and demerits of judges from various old pros of one's acquaintance. The neophyte is assured that THIS all-rounder NEVER puts up his type of dog, whereas THAT judge ALWAYS goes for a female handler. The OTHER judge doesn't know a dog from a goat and will always put up the first one into the ring. And then there are the oceans of grooming tips from the various schools of thought, ranging from the super-natural to the super-artificial.

It takes years of trial and error, mostly the latter, to acquire just the right collection of showgoing gear. By the time it is all collected, it is usually a garage full to say the least, what with crates, dollies, tack boxes, folding chairs, umbrellas, picnic coolers, awnings for the van or wagon, water jugs, exercise pens, and stake outs. Then there are the untold masses of mysterious spray cans and bottles, lotions and powders, bait, leashes, combs, brushes, towels and assorted tools of the trade. Each person owning even ONE small, mediocre show prospect seems to plunge into it at first with the zeal of a fanatic, having the urge to possess EVERYTHING even remotely connected with the dog game, whether needed or not. One must equip as for an African safari, for after all, it is BIG GAME!

Occasionally you will see an old timer, blasé and calm, going to his two-millionth show with a small bag containing one comb and a show lead. But this type is definitely in the minority. There is something about a dog show that brings out the pack rat in all participants. Not only do they tend to ARRIVE at the show laden down like oxen on the frontier trail, but they seem to be driven to ACQUIRE even MORE dog oriented paraphernalia AT the shows, patronizing the concessions and coming away with more grooming aids, more leashes, more decals, note paper, figurines of their beloved breed, and other absolutely necessary things that can be added to the general dogginess of their homes and lives.

The average show-goer starts preparing for shows far in advance, not only out of necessity to prepare coats and generally condition the dogs, but to arrange the household. They also make advance plans, alert fellow-show-goers, arrange trysts, book motels and much else that takes up most of the preceding week. The real zealot packs the car the night before, forgetting NOTHING. Even things that will never be needed are packed, but every exhibitor knows that you never can tell about weather, accommodations, sudden ailments or changes of plans, not to mention car trouble and the like.

On arriving at the show, be it outdoors or indoors, there is the terrible trauma of the last minute arrival. The cars and people create a tie-up getting in, and ALWAYS your class is imminent; and there are hundreds of fellow exhibitors all bottlenecked trying to get in at the same time.

And then come the blind staggers, when you are finally out of the car and underway with the vast gear all piled on top of the dolly, under which pile is your prize hopeful, barking insanely at all the other dogs who are also riding in on THEIR dollies, piled high with show gear. Someone is frantically trying to stamp your hand, and someone else is trying to sell you a catalog; and several friends and one or two enemies are also jostling by trying to get in at the same time. This is inevitably when your folding chair slips and crashes into a crate and starts a new pandemonium of barking ... or your tack box falls on your toe.

But eventually you are installed in some remote spot, far from your ring, jammed up against some professional handlers who are lost in a cloud of powder and spray. Your dog may have been neatly toweled but by now has gotten wet, or worse, the safety pin has become jammed never to be extricated. By some miracle, you are at last ready for the ring, after having set up your ex-pen (if it's summer) and being told it's illegal; or perhaps (if it's summer) the tent has just dropped several gallons of cold water down the back of your best garment.

Naturally, when you have dashed to your ring, you find that ALL the other exhibitors are professional handlers. They have ALL just gotten there ahead of you and you are the last in the ring. On top of this, your dog has stopped to scoot its rear along the ground in mute testimony of either worms or anal gland trouble. You don't make a grand entrance.

If it's an indoor show, the mats are inadequate, generally; and you have on new, slippery shoes. At most outdoor shows, you get to pose your dog in a depression in the grass giving your hopeful a rather DIFFERENT topline. Just as you are about to make your big presentation and gait your best, the show photographer goes to work in the next ring, all hung over with cameras like a tourist in Europe, throwing up squeaky toys, etc., that so distract your dog that he walks sidewise and backward during the entire gaiting pattern.

More often than not, all is lost. You can come out of the ring to mutter with the other sadder and wiser exhibitors about the inadequate judge. This is the one balm that the losers have left, that comforting thought that the judge REALLY doesn't know the breed, and he is REALLY prejudiced, and so on, ad nauseam.

So, back to the crate, and by this time your tack box has been knocked over by the next-door cratee and the contents all muddled. Your Mr. Groom

spray inside has become compressed and sprayed the entire interior of the tack box, gumming up your show leads, old ribbons, and freeze-dried liver. There's nothing to do at this point but make a tour of the show and cheer yourself up by buying a whole lot of doggy items to make you feel better. Some new grooming aids are sure to turn the trick next time; a new type of lead and maybe several books on handling are snapped up. In any case, one MUST buy. In the case of a nice win, on the other hand, it is essential that you rush about and buy a lot of things to treat yourself and sort of celebrate!

And, of course, even if the kennel, cellar or garage is full of a thousand pounds of dog food, one never leaves the show without all the samples one can carry of the various biscuits and kibbles that the salesmen press on us all. And lastly, win or lose, one must eat, patronizing the food concessions and/or one's own picnic provender, for, as the saying goes, "When all else fails, EAT!" This fills in waiting spaces nicely and gives you something to do with your hands when they're not on your dog.

From Riches to Bitches

Once in a blue moon some devotee goes to a dog show WITHOUT a dog. Possibly the ones hitherto being campaigned are either in whelp, all finished (whoopee!), or out of coat, or perhaps the judge is just too much to deal with. But the pull of the show is too strong; so, like the old circus horse when the music sounds, out goes the dog-shower to go through the paces yet again. This is a fine time to watch all your friends' dogs when you are relaxed and at ease, invariably noting what rotten specimens they really are now that you have the time to actually concentrate on them and haven't a dog of your own to worry about. And you can really observe how inadequate the judges are, and how sneaky the professional handlers are with their evil tricks, and how unsportsmanlike all the other contestants are. It is a field day for the dogless show-goer to be critical and eagle-eyed. He usually comes away feeling quite prepared to be a judge himself at the very least, if not an AKC rep.

This is also a fine time to stand back and observe the passing scene in a way impossible when one is PART of that scene. In the matter of dress, one's fellow man often leaves much to be desired; and never is it so apparent as at a dog show. Summer shows really tend to bring out the most ludicrous in people. With the exception of professional handlers (the majority of whom dress conservatively and blend with the background), most exhibitors seem to feel they must put on a better show than their dogs to gain the acclaim of the judges and the gallery. Every last handler seems to know intuitively what is best for the presentation of his DOG; but as to his own "plumage" ... well, it's anything goes and the less suitable to the face and figure, the better!

The breed people often go in for "costumes," so to speak, some becoming but others appalling. Obedience people are a rather different breed of cat and often proclaim their difference in a more "it's-all-for-the-sport-of-the-thing" attitude, which can add up to the super-casual. On the whole, the men come off better than the ladies, though some male members do put on quite a show. But the ladies (all of whom can, of course, judge a dog with a keen eye) often have not judged their own conformation equally as well! But it's all in the pageantry of the show, and what's a show without tight pants, miniskirts, flowing garb, poured-into suits, blue jeans and sun suits? The wigs, rain gear, weird footgear, and the vanity license plates that spell out some cutesy thing relative to YOUR doggie are all part of the contemporary scene. The fantastic recreational vehicles wending their way over miles of highways, guzzling gas, to get your canine money-burners to their appointments with destiny are fast-becoming the way to go. Every weekend, off go the dog devotees, leaving loved ones, progeny, jobs and homes, pilgrimaging after the elusive points and ribbons, trophies and "legs." The only ones not totally and 100% gung-ho may be the dogs, who usually take it a bit ho-hum but cheerfully go along to keep the boss happy.

Then finally, after eons, it seems, comes THE show with the final

the perils of owner-handling

points that spell NEW CHAMPION. Or maybe it's a Best of Breed and a Group win, and you handled your winner YOURSELF! And suddenly all the dog people emerge as the GREAT GUYS they really are, shaking your hand and planting kisses. The judge, after all, is the MOST perceptive and knowledgeable of canine experts. Everyone is your good buddy, and even your long-time rivals seem good fellows this great day. Perhaps a breeder sidles up to you surreptitiously to suggest a stud service, like a purveyor of French postcards. It's YOUR day, and plans are make for a gala championship champagne party and another celebration in the near future and naturally a repeat breeding! The fog of euphoria mercifully obscures the memories of other shows when you were lucky to emerge from the ring with a fourth out of four. So it's all worthwhile, and you hurry back home to the puppy pen to pick out another career canine to brighten golden dog show days that lie ahead.

Dedication Raised to an Art Form

T he zeal and dedication of dog devotees surpasseth all understanding. Overheard recently at a dog club meeting: First member, musing over the *Gazette,* "Well, I'm planning to go to the Wumpalunk show. Are you?"

Second member: "Yes, but that's Easter Sunday, so I'll have to do some careful arranging. Someone will have to get the family to church on time, and maybe my husband can manage the microwave for a simple dinner."

First member: "I've told my family to send out for Kentucky Fried Chicken and read a passage from the Bible over it. I'm GOING! Anyway they won't miss me. I've been at a show every Easter and Mother's Day for ten years."

Second member: "MY family is still muttering over the time I went

SHOW BIZ

on the the Round Heel Circuit and delivered my mother-in-law to the hospital emergency room laid out on top of dog crates on the way."

First member: "I recall that! How narrow and selfish families can get sometimes! Like when I was on the Crotched Mountain circuit and getting majors every day, and my family expected me to come back when my husband was in that car smash up."

Second member: "That was the time you took the new van and left him with the Volkswagen with no brakes?"

First member: "Hmmm ... yes, well that WAS a bad scene ... but it was a worse one when Helen Hairshirt left her daughter's wedding reception to breed a bitch in the hotel ladies room; and the guests made a scene when the stud dog bit a lady in one of the booths; and then he ran out and chewed on the wedding cake."

Third member, coming up and joining in: "Oh, I remember that time! They had a two minute tie just the same and had eleven puppies!"

Second member: "Are you going to the Skunk Hollow Kennel Club show this weekend?"

Third member: "I sure am! But it'll be a hassle at home because that's my uncle's funeral. He was 97, but he loved dogs; so I'm sure he'd be happy for me. But if I don't get the points, I may rush home for the reading of the will."

Second member: "That reminds me of Marvin Marrowbone; you remember him. He had his heart set on the Specialty at Moldy Lake, and then his wife died. He canceled the family plot plans, and had the funeral at a cemetery next to the show grounds in the morning, and still made it into Open Bitch class later."

Third member: "Yes, he was very dedicated."

From Riches to Bitches

First member: "Well, no more so than the Dysplacias, you know, Dave and Diana. When she was expecting, they went out on the Trashberry Circuit down south; and she had her baby in the van. Dave was in the ring at the time."

Fourth member arriving: "My company is giving me a retiring party at the Giltrock Hilton with a gold watch and the works, and I'm entered in the Gasping Creek Kennel Club that day! What a dilemma!"

All the other members: "Well, George, you KNOW there's no choice! What THAT judge and YOUR bitch who needs a gold watch!"

Random Musings

Muse awhile on how to get to the obscure dog show where the location changes every year due to disasters, excessive tire marks on the grounds, building development, or too much N.O.M. (natural organic material).

The show superintendent's directions appear to have been copied from a 1911 road atlas. Furthermore, it gives the complicated formula for routing to the show from north, south, east, but YOU are approaching from the WEST, so must read the east directions in reverse.

This brings you through a major metropolis where the route you are following mysteriously disappears amid the bowels of the city, where you then spend a precious and nerve-fraught hour backing and filling, turning and reversing, all at 7 a.m. on a Sunday morning when NOTHING is open and no humans are on the streets to inquire of ... except one elderly lady going to early Mass who speaks no English.

Eventually you find one 24-hour bistro open with truck drivers and dubious characters within. You can tell it's "class" all the way – from the painting on black velvet of bug-eyed horses to the one of Christ hovering over a diesel truck. But they have NEVER heard of the show grounds! Which isn't too surprising since this year's new and glorious location is the Czechoslovakian Athletic and Marching Society's new clubhouse.

After more frenetic driving, tempers are frayed and several two- and four-footed passengers are needing "comfort" stops; suddenly, salvation is seen! Like Columbus spotting a landfall, we spot a red and white "dog-show" arrow, nailed at a crazy angle to a telegraph pole, pointing, alas, in the general direction of the ground, leaving everyone puzzled since it is an intersection.

However, several more miles, some reversing and two wrong turns produces still another welcome dog-show sign, thus raising high hopes. But doubts assail as the road becomes ever more rural, finally changing to a dirt track, then terminating in a huge field with wilderness surrounding a clubhouse of rustic type.

It is soon apparent that, signs notwithstanding, we have reached not the elusive show, but a Beagle trial ... and by our reckoning we are already well on the way to being VERY late for our class. After a conference with the Beagle personnel, it seems best to backtrack to the center of town and start fresh. Just as all seems lost and the map is shredded and everyone is "back-seat driving" – even the dogs – and blaming the other fellow's rotten sense of direction, WE ARE THERE! Well, almost – for we are in a long line of cars and vans and trailers, all snailing along to the show entrance where several short-tempered policemen have already had enough of the dog fanciers and are routing the biggest campers to the swamp and the Volkswagens over the rockiest areas. In vain you scream that you MUST unload, and you finally do, and the rest is history that you can write yourself, according to whether your dog was Best of Breed that day or a flustered, ungroomed no-show.

You can bet it'll happen again, of course ...

Do the dogs understand words and phrases? Some say no, but who knows ... HA! Picture the scene:

Evening. Everyone is deep in concentration behind newspapers. All dogs are sacked out on the best couch cover, beanbag chair, and other choice places, leaving humans to make do with backbreaking antique Boston rockers and horsehair loveseats, etc. Silence.

Someone says, low voiced, "Well, the mid-east oil situation isn't getting any better ..."

Other person, suddenly alert, and in a very high voice, "What's happening?"

Instantly this key phrase alerts every canine within earshot. All leap out of dreamland, half-oriented, yelping.

"YEAH! What's happening ... who? What? Where? Shall we catch an intruder? Is it supper? Company? What ... who ... bark, bark, bark ..."

End to intellectual evening.

OR: When the long-lost second cousin comes after a 40-year absence from family ties. Old family photos are brought out and a reunion is taking place; BUT, somehow one finds dog-oriented comments creeping in ...

"Now here's a photo of Aunt Flora and Uncle Fred and that poor specimen of a Beagle ... just look at that front ..."

"Oh, yes ... Uncle Fred does look like your husband ..."

"I guess it's line-breeding ..."

One cannot seem to eliminate the doggy talk and references. They infiltrate no matter what.

"Do have another brownie ... (musingly) Ah, yes, that's the silver tray they're on that old Fonzo won when he went Best of Breed over 27 specials at the Wumpalug Kennel Club in '62 ..."

Then maybe it's an effort to refrain from references to places visited when one hasn't seen a relative in many years ...

"Oh! So your oldest son is in Delaware now. Lovely ... I remember our specialty was there in Wilmington in '64, or was it '66 ..." or maybe: "Oh, yes, I've heard it's interesting in Pensacola. I recall my dear bitch Crumsie went on that circuit in '71 and finished with nine majors."

About this time, of course, the second cousin plans the next visit in about 40 years, probably at your funeral ...

Random Observations

Ah, the vagaries of fate. One wonders what two top all-breed judges must feel at the conclusion of a weekend where both judge almost identical assignments and not one placement agreed. This must be akin to the situation in which a gentleman pays two genealogy firms to trace his roots. After both firms delve deeply and engage in very extensive research, they trace him back to two totally unrelated families and all peasant stock. The owners of all the dogs shown under the two judges can be up one day and down the next. All this leads to troubled nights spent worrying which judge is right, which judge is wrong, who to have faith in, what judge to ever trust again, or whether they should sell their dogs.

Moments designed to deflate: You've just used a well advertised dishwashing liquid on your vast collection of trophy glasses won over the years at different shows. The dazzling spotlessness highlights the breed motifs and club logos. Irresistible! WRONG! A neato guest wants water with which to take a pill. He ignores the array of glasses and chooses one old jelly glass recently used for rooting a plant, all slime and glop, that you forgot to toss out.

I'm not one to spout on women's rights and probably would not have been a suffragette way back then. However, have you ever noticed in a totally doggy household it DOES seem as if the woman gets to do most of the main steering? Sometimes, as evidenced by some cases I've known, George isn't always lighting the fire with the right end of the match. He is the one who goes out, grumbling and half-oriented, to gather the stool samples in little labeled baggies. He collects the samples but gets them all mixed up and doesn't own up to it until the wrong dogs have been treated for the wrong worms. He is the one who asked to take care of that puddle, absently applies one Kleenex over the spot and sprays a hiss of air spray and goes blithely back to the sport page. On the rare Sundays when you are not at a dog show and go to church, HE isn't the one to get spiritual nourishment. He elects to stay home and read the paper over a non-stop breakfast, steadily feeding forbidden tidbits to all the fat dogs.

Once You're in Utility

Once you have a utility obedience dog, you MAY have the perfect dog genius. On the other hand, you may have created a lovable canine Frankenstein. Having carefully and patiently taught your dog to make the very most of his brain power, he may continue to use it in a way somewhat resembling a clever semi-criminal, but one of those whose crimes are never vicious, just somehow admirable for their sheer inventiveness and self-advancement.

With four UDT's and another in training, I am finding myself losing my grip on canine matters as the accumulated dog brain power continues to grow. Results may seldom show up in the ring, where all too often the glazed eye and lagging step show that this is an "off day" for doggy concentration.

But around home the UDT type dog is quite a challenge to out-think. Cricket, UDT, is squirrel-oriented, having been brought up on Boston Common where one stumbles over the fat and sassy creatures on every dog walk. This mad and insatiable passion has never left my Cricket, only to be fanned anew when she actually caught a wintering-in-the-attic resident who emerged from a closet.

Since then much of Cricket's time is spent policing the bedrooms, lying immobile and trembling by cracks in the baseboard and under beds. The two guest rooms are kept closed, but it is her great ambition to get in as she is sure that the best squirrels are holed up in there.

On one illustrious occasion, a guest room was opened for a visitor and in went our UDT, snuffling busily under the bed. In the confusion, no one noticed; and the door was again closed. Everyone left for the movies, and Cricket was not missed. At 11 p.m. the dogs were all called for the evening outing, but no Cricket appeared; a thorough search revealed no sign of her. Everyone, fearful of dognappers, scattered about the neighborhood calling, to no avail. Eventually the guest-room door, now closed, was tried. It was locked! Was Cricket within? Always the most talkative dog, with a truly phenomenal vocabulary of whines, growls, grumbles and other dog language, Cricket was now silent; that is, IF she was in there.

After another search of the premises, careful listening at the keyhole revealed a rustling in the mysterious locked room. Must be Cricket! No key for the Yale lock had ever been remembered since my grandfather's day, so the only obvious solution was entrance through the upstairs window. Since it was then midnight, it was a sticky problem how to get Cricket OUT and weary guests installed. An apologetic phone call was made to a neighbor, who was in his pajamas about to retire. He listened silently to the unlikely story ... ("That dog nut has got one of her mutts locked in a bedroom!" he probably said to his wife, tapping his forehead.) He agreed to dress and get his ladder and come over. At 1 a.m. the ladder was being steadied in its precarious base of deep snow and crusted ice. The hardy neighbor was cutting off a last-summer's screen that no one had ever removed, and which, naturally, could only be unscrewed from the inside.

Cricket, tongue lolling in a wide grin, was happily beating on the windowpane, the rescued maiden-at-the-tower-window! Once the window was opened, she complicated matters by getting in the carnival spirit of things, lapping the rescuer's face exuberantly and trying to climb OUT which, of course, gave the assembled onlookers heart failure.

It was discovered that she had put her fiendish paw on the lock button. How? Who will ever know, but she'd been doing it in cars for years, so she was in practice. She had made a rat's nest of the best bedspread in her hours of incarceration, but had probably been so engrossed in silent squirreling that she never minded the time passing or cared about the anguish of her humans. All that mattered was that at long last, by fair means or foul, she had managed several hours of uninterrupted squirreling in a forbidden room. She won. She always does (except at some shows).

The other two educated dogs are also studying up for their degree in master criminology. Crispy, probably the most food-oriented dog in the USA, Canada and Bermuda, can detect with uncanny accuracy any edible fragment, be it birdseed embedded in a concrete wall. Despite endless chastisement, she

The Long Long Sit...

An Obedience episode: the "3 minute Long Sit."

rifles wastebaskets, but of course, NEVER when observed. Only when humans are otherwise occupied are the cans and containers skillfully plucked out and hidden in the depths of the dog bed.

To purloin a phrase from some forgotten and marvelous dog book, this dog could sleep calmly through a collision of major planets, yet from the far reaches of the house or yard can easily detect the soundless opening of the refrigerator door. Before one can hardly have time to scan the contents, like a darting trout she slips between ankles and grabs at whatever is on the nearest shelf. Nine times out of ten it is a successful coup, as ham, butter, or steak goes disappearing around the corner and down the gullet. Sometimes it is a casserole dish, which is neatly grabbed in teeth, overturned, and contents gobbled in a twinkling. For this reason a riding crop hangs by the refrigerator door, and one is forewarned never to attempt an opening without a weapon in hand.

Utility for some dogs is soon boring in class and a chore in the ring, but it is a great exerciser of brain power for latent juvenile delinquency along lines only a smart operator dog can conjure up. After years of the "seek-back," "directed retrieve," and work with the tracking glove, my canine masterminds are now also GLOVE-oriented, feeling that somehow gloves are a form of canine currency to be collected at all costs and by any means, usually dishonest, and later exchanged for praise and goodies.

Driving gloves in other people's cars are particularly choice. Garden gloves must always be stowed away in hidden places, later to be brought to light. Fur lined gloves, the gold pieces of dogdom, must have the fur removed first and buried in the dog bed, if not eaten, before later barter.

A good Utility dog no longer really chews up shoes, of course, but mine feel that all projections such as buckles, bows and straps should be removed, and all left shoes should be pushed as far under beds as possible. All old bones must be hidden in bedclothes, too. After all, retrieving odd objects has been well learned!

Once advanced to Utility rank, there's no end of chores that a good dog can perform. Cricket habitually carries letters, notes, paper bags of small objects, small books, etc., up and down stairs, to and from her humans, thus saving many a step. Also it is her job to greet the newsboys at the gate and bring back the paper neatly, which she does with a few barks to show her superiority over small boys, then some amazing wagging calisthenics. All this EXCEPT, of course, on days when OTHER owners of UD dogs come to visit, upon which occasions she hurls dirty epithets at the newsboy, snatches the paper on the 52nd command, opens it, drops and scrambles it several times, and finally deposits it in the birdbath during a slurping drink.

There are just so many times that a good UDT dog MUST assert individuality to keep balance between himself and owner, perhaps to pay back the long standing debt for all those grueling hours of class and ring work. So watch it when you try for a UDT!

The Coldnose County KC Jubilee Show

After much negotiating with the American Kennel Club and several years of preparations, the Coldnose County Kennel Club at long last held its prestigious and utterly notable Jubilee show. This long awaited extravaganza took place on a vast tract of land leased for the event from the Utilities Company, who had earmarked it for a huge nuclear plant.

A first among firsts, this canine bonanza offered five days of events, covering every possible phase of the canine sport. Practically EVERY breed club held its specialty in conjunction, with a resulting chaos of special tents, chicken barbecues, ox-roasts, buffets and celebrations. Motels and campgrounds for miles around put up cots under trees, and the Johnny-on-the-spot outfits were forced to hastily nail up old time one-holers. The entire town ran out of toilet paper by noon, and the Board of Health officials were in a state of shock. All was in merry chaos.

The gate was enormous as the general public flocked in, curiosity piqued by giant neon billboards, to see the Whippet races, and the Greyhound coursing, and other events. Federal agents and the local gestapo scurried about frantically trying to stop ringside betting at the races while SPCA men fanned out, searching vans for jackrabbits the Greyhound people might have smuggled in. During the Whippet races, several contestants mistook the course and bolted through the entire showgrounds in pursuit of a Chihuahua. All were located later at a Howard Johnson's on the interstate highway.

Many foreign visitors were on hand, among them lots of small Japanese staggering under the weight of multiple cameras and offering to buy the Group winners. Elderlies, club charter members, lounged in wheelchairs under the hospitality tent, reminiscing over their Gin and Geritols.

The two AKC reps supplied for this monster event collapsed during

The Banquet Lecture

the course of duty trying to keep the tangled skeins of dog problems straightened out, and finally both went off to a local pub to compose requests for transfers to AKC Show Records Department desk jobs.

The tracking was somewhat blighted since several horsemen, a woodchuck, and a fox ran across all ten fields. Those exhibitors in attendance voted to be good sports and carry on anyway, but all dogs failed, some going down chuck holes, some into the cool pond, and one Yorkshire Terrier caught the fox!

The terrier trails somehow got fouled up as the area overlapped the working dog tests for spaniels. A number of English Cockers buried their pigeons in the terrier earth-runs; one Springer carried a muskrat into the pond, and an American Cocker got tangled in his own hair down a terrier tunnel. He then met a Norwich coming out, and both adversaries came out poorly ...

The gala club hospitality party the night before had taken its toll on all club officers and workers, as well as the majority of judges, most of whom stumbled about at the show glassyeyed and queasy, carrying out assignments in a daze. Most of the judges were honorary oldtimer all-rounders, and many had grave difficulty bending down to locate the small dogs.

The Utility ring was adjacent to the chicken barbecue, and several contestants rose into the air for the bar jump, tested the wind, and sailed off for the chicken tent ... (English Cockers all!)

The weather, appropriately for such a diversified event, served up a great variety of conditions beginning in early morning with a fog so dense that several early comers fell over tent ropes, dropping huge crates on their toes. Several tracklayers were totally lost after laying tracks overlapping on each other.

As the day progressed, the intense heat sent everyone to well-stocked coolers for the cup that cheers; and a troop of fifty Boy Scouts were on the run gathering up the empties. All was still chaos.

By midday, severe winds blew down one tent and uprooted another, flattening several famous professional handlers who were putting the finishing touches on some Bichons. This was followed by torrential, brief thundershowers which thoroughly soaked the handlers and their supergroomed dogs, which then emerged as the chicken-chested runts they really were. All humanity was sent scrambling under tents where the crowding caused several faintings and one broken arm.

As the weather cleared leaving a morass of mud, the sled-dog demonstration sunk into the muck and had to be hauled out by some Newfoundlands, occasioning a nasty dog melee.

The first of the Great Exodus began as the sore losers packed up to depart, shredding their Reserve ribbons. All tow trucks in town were summoned to haul the unfortunate vans and campers out of the mud and swamps. Several were abandoned forever, presumably, to sink slowly into patches of quicksand.

As the Groups progressed to Best in Show (won by a Jugoslavian Charplaninatz shepherd dog) officials from AKC were seen in violent altercations with the owners of the grounds, (now a ruin) and the by-now-zombie club officers. The show chairman had already been taken away ...

As the sun set, and the Boss-Moe trucks rumbled in through the mud, roustabouts grimly surveyed a vast sea of dog groomings and debris. All agreed that the Coldnose County Kennel Club's Jubilee show was a historic event, never, it is to be hoped, repeated.

Corresponding Secretary,
Penelope Pooperscooper

Coldnose County KC Annual Banquet

The Coldnose County Kennel Club held its annual banquet last week at the Hair and Hounds Restaurant. Club President, J. Waldo Sport, famous importer of Australian Whippersnappers, presided at the head table. Some substance from the kennel adhering to his shoe lent a familiar air to the atmosphere, starting the evening on a note of informality. The president's wife, attired in a hand-woven Afghan fur shift, wore her famous Afro wig of Poodle clippings.

Club Treasurer Pilchington Piggybank read the annual financial report from the backs of old Purina armbands, coming up with an unsettling balance to be presented later to a CPA for further study.

Our obedience trainer of many years, Frank Forwardhalt, arrived a bit late via wheelchair, nursing an infected Chihuahua bite on the ankle, as well as a fracture on the other foot from a falling bar jump.

Show Chairman Agatha Boomer-Moxie outlined plans for the forthcoming point show to be held this year in the parking lot of the local shopping mall and supermarket. Winners will be awarded coupons entitling them to either steaks or gas or even aluminum foil trophies, thus the Trophy Committee reported a great savings on engraving.

A tattoo clinic will be offered, with an added bonus of intertwined hearts with every third tattoo. This year, owners may have their dogs' registration numbers tattooed on any appropriate portion of their own anatomies in case of streaking plans.

Top professional handler Winifred Winnersbitch drove in at the last moment from a circuit in upper Saskatchewan having shown her rare Abominable Snowdog to Best in Show.

Longtime AKC Delegate, Colonel Ascarid, was finally located in the lounge bar and managed to give his report before slowly sinking into his Lobster Newburg.

A moment's silence was observed for two members who are now, it is to be hoped, getting points in that Great Show in the Sky: Miss Gladys Gainesburger was lost in a bog while tracking; she is survived by her Italian Spumoni which completed the track. Mr. Lester Livasnap is presumed lost inside AKC. Both are gone, but not forgotten.

Annual awards were presented to a total of 69 members for varying achievements, notable among them Mrs. Angus MacKilt's Scottish Deerhound which had 27 puppies, unfortunately from a misalliance with her UDT Basset. Completed CDs, CDXs and UDs, as well as championships, were awarded trophies in the form of pewter boxes cleverly designed to hold the recipients' future welfare checks.

The speaker of the evening was well-known area veterinarian, Dr. David Dewclaw, who spoke on anal glands, stool specimens, and worms. He

"They say they want 152 doggy bags...."

was introduced by Vice-President Agnes Alpo, in place of the President who was retching quietly into his napkin. Glass specimen tubes were passed around with only one casualty during the dessert course.

The meeting came to a close with an X-rated film entitled "Management of the Stud Dog" which caught the attention of all present. Another banner year for Coldnose County!

Corresponding Secretary,
Penelope Pooperscooper

Tales of a Communal Trauma

News of the Coldnose County Kennel Club has surfaced again. This time the entire membership of this venerable group was (for the first time since 1929) in unanimous accord at a recent meeting when an article from a national dog magazine was read and discussed. A well-known dog person had pointed out (and how truly) that the dog fancier would do well to aim for a more balanced life, to have other interests – to diversify. The article claimed it is unhealthy to be so blindly dedicated to the dog sport to the point where one's perspective becomes hopelessly warped.

Each CCKC member, in a rare display of clear-sightedness, admitted that there was room for a bit of a new life-style. They resolved that vigorous efforts should be mounted immediately to seek oneself in the great world that lies beyond the show ring.

Agnes Alpo, President, announced that she would begin on the spot and cast the first stone. Valiantly, Agnes promptly tore ALL the felt dog appliqués from her jacket and tossed them to the floor in a most dramatic gesture – sobbing as she did so. Not to be outdone, Lester Livasnap threw his hand-carved meerschaum pipe into the trash barrel. This was the familiar old pipe whose bowl was carved into the shape of a Bulldog head and was a prized possession of Lester's since he was old enough to smoke!

Warming to the spirit, David DeBark wrenched off innumerable insignias and gundog club badges from his genuine Austrian hat and even divested it of its jaunty pheasant feather. Ambrose Armband kept the tempo going by suggesting everyone replace their dog oriented bumper stickers with new ones that say "Acupuncture Is the Point," "I Brake for Rolling Stones," "Warning: Tattooed Children," "Love Is a Hairless Rug," "National Gerbil Racing Team," "Sex Is Old-Fashioned," and "Have You Hugged Your Parakeet Today?"

Ambrose then moved that club members attempt a four-month phasing out of the excesses of dog-centered devotion and adopt other balancing factors in their respective life styles. The motion carried, and everyone filed out like pallbearers at a funeral, choking on the brownies, and grimly trying to believe that in four months they would all be more well-rounded members of the human race.

In the ensuing months, great efforts were made, judging from all reports; but the overall picture was not bright.

Several members left immediately on overseas trips, vowing NOT to call home daily to check on the dogs and not to leave with the kennel sitter their every-night hotel address. None had memorable trips. In England, Victor Vetbill spent most of his time in pubs, staring fixedly at the advertising pictures of the Scottie and Westie in the Black and White Scotch posters. Mavis Monorchid went AWOL from her charter tours several times and was found sobbing and clutching at the fence of the nearest quarantine kennel.

Mr. and Mrs. Rudolph Rugpuddle decided to go all out and redecorate, and called in professionals who, after initial shudders, finally agreed to do over the entire house. Eventually prying off clutching fingers from 2,567 framed 8x10 photos and certificates on the walls, they did the whole house over. They replaced those sacred dog show mementos with contemporary prints, collages and woven hangings. Of course, the walls had to be replastered due to the 2,567 nail holes. The unadjusted homeowners later slipped backward more and more in their resolve, creeping down to the tool shed to pore over the old photos and certificates. At each trip, they smuggled back JUST ONE to hang in the john or some empty spot.

Sarah Sittandown made a clean sweep of her houseful of old trophies, which couldn't be melted down as so many were just cheap metal. But the whole batch went to the local nursing home to be used for flower containers. Sarah spent much time frantically visiting the old folks at Geriatric Gardens, tenderly touching her Best of Breed trophies and sometimes bringing in the silver polish.

Several older members, somewhat housebound and less active, took up needlepoint madly, after storing several tons of old dog magazines in their attics so they would have the time to work at the replacement activity. Eventually they got tired of doing their grandchildren's faces for the purpose of gracing chair seats. It didn't seem quite right to devote all that effort to a project that only resulted in visitors sitting on one's posterity.

Florence Fleaspray had what started out as a good idea. She resolutely sewed together all her old ribbons into a vast and colorful quilt. This she donated to her church as the grand prize in a special raffle. Alas, the idea turned sour when Florence's resolve weakened, and she bought up every available ticket at a cost of $700; of course, she won the quilt and experienced guilt feelings every day when she went to the bottom drawer of the bureau to secretly stroke the quilt.

Carolyn Call-Cornell opted for a class in aerobics. She bought a body suit and whatever else she needed, but quit in a tearful blubber when the instructor undiplomatically observed that she moved like a Basset Hound.

The Clipperburns, Claude and Connie, took up jogging and bicycling respectively, but were forced to discontinue these healthful avocations. This was due to the large number of dog bites they suffered and the unvarying aftermath. They found themselves getting into long conversations with the owners about behavior conditioning and obedience classes – totally nonproductive and the bites often were painful.

Like most of the other struggling members, Malcolm Malocclusion found something new to occupy his mind and his energies. He got into archaeology – picking up on an old interest from his high school and college years. Unfortunately, this didn't work any better for Malcolm than the other alternate hobbies did for the others. It seems Malcolm got broody when all he could turn up were old bones buried by older dogs. Archaeology was then given up as a bad job.

Several CCKC members resolved to devote themselves much more to their families, especially to their children. One woman began crating her three-year-old and another decided it would be cute if her twins could work as a brace and began training them accordingly. Several even went so far as to join the PTA but quit shortly thereafter, claiming the lack of trophies robbed organization projects of incentive.

A number of other members turned to the finer things for their dog-less diversion. They got together and joined the Coldnose County Culture Society to avail themselves of many varied offerings of this noteworthy organization. Opera, concerts, art, and flower shows were but a sampling of what was available. Unfortunately, canine-free, culturally balanced conversation was difficult to achieve within the group. Beethoven was crowded by Bulldogs, and Mozart lost ground to Mastiffs. During the art shows, Rembrandt was often eclipsed by Rottweilers, while the gorgeous azaleas being displayed at the flower show went unnoticed in favor of Airedales. During the highly successful Debussy concert, one of the reformed dog clubbers absentmindedly doodled dogs on her program. By intermission, the subject's program was totally unreadable.

As the weeks wore on, it was evident that brains bore the permanent impression of pawprints, even though it was reported that a few license plates were changed back from BOWWOW and WOOF to things like the rich uncle's birth date and other legends designed to yield special dividends at some future time.

At the end of the four-month trial period, a sadder, yet wiser group of CCKC members came together to evaluate the experiment. It was reluctantly admitted that the effort was something less than a total success, and a vote was carried to shelve any extension of the project for at least ten years. At that point, pandemonium erupted as at least half the members in attendance whipped out huge folders of Polaroid snapshots. As they happily cooed over the pictures of each others' newest puppies, they had to shout over the din they were also contributing to. The frenzied conversation ran the gamut from planning breedings and new and imminent litters to new diet regimens, supplements, and obedience methods.

During this joyful renewal, several dogs that had accompanied their owners to the meeting, ate ALL the refreshments; and, after chewing up the Secretary's minutes for the last two years, began on the cashbox. Nobody seemed to mind as they chalked up another crisis faced and resolved for Coldnose County.

Plans are now well underway for a totally new event, since CCKC has thrown in the whole towel on alternate life-styles and may well become the first-ever canine holistic society. So watch for CCKC's gala Spring show, featuring a flea market, arts and crafts festival, doggy bake boutique, jiffy dog wash and MORE. There are to be 77 concessions and new things to experience — such as canine palmistry (pawistry), horoscopes and tarot readings. Everything will be on the same grounds, too. A MUST! For the two-pound premium list, write Penelope Pooperscooper, Secretary.

V.
Ties that Bind
The Favorite

As my grandmother used to say when asked which of her children was her favorite, "Whichever one is sick, in trouble or needs me." So it is here. Maybe it's the old-timer who has me and the vet worrying about a suspicious lump that, alas, is growing. The favorite could be the bitch having a difficult time whelping, or the languishing, tiny puppy being tube-fed, but not gaining very well. Even though this wee one has no discernible personality yet, there is valiant courage in those infant eyes turning mutely to you for help and comfort. Somehow it melts you down. How could this babe not be a favorite?

When the brave hunter returns home staggering with the excruciating pain of a face full of porcupine quills, he qualifies as the favorite. Likewise, the Middle Dog, who is neither the best-loved oldster or the most fussed over young one, but seems to grieve, nose on paws with neglect, could stand a turn as a favorite. And it's the same study in pathos for the retired champion UDT who has run out of worlds to conquer. This one will often be found in the upstairs den, moping over lead and dumbbell, symbols of bygone triumph, like an aging ballerina mourning over her old ballet shoes.

The favorite could be the one who is off her feed and has some strange malady as yet undiagnosed. You always worry about the mysterious diseases science has no research on as yet. Then there's the dog that is VERY SICK, and even if is only a passing upset (and she was riotous yesterday and will be tomorrow ...) surely, SHE is your favorite!

Also actively contending for favorite is the insecure soul who trots up to you at least 500 times a day with her precious tattered frog for you to throw. This can be at dinnertime, bedtime – ANYTIME! And if you don't throw the frog and praise her everytime she retrieves it, she will develop a trauma. Right along with the frog retriever is the snack freak. This one has the infallible facility of locating the biscuit box. It doesn't matter in what new or secret place you've hidden the edibles, or how many times you have moved them ... she'll find 'em, sometimes before you do. So, like the frog retriever, the snack freak deserves favorite status, too.

And the one who comes home from a show the winner may be your temporary favorite, but more attention must be lavished on the loser. Maybe the dog was the unwitting victim of bad judging and must be given solace and encouragement to face the next outing.

Lastly, through the years, it is ever the same, no matter what. It is always the one who finally passes on who is unquestionably your very favorite, never to be replaced. And this remains true unto the 90th dog or the 900th. Each is irreplaceable, but each new dog is an entirely independent personality – a whole fresh soul – waiting in the wings for his or her day of being your special favorite and the joy of top dog status.

Fortunately the dog person's heart is ever expandable.

Food and Special Diet

'T is stated in the Bible that man cannot live by bread alone. How true this is, I often think, as I go through the supermarket perusing the two million acres of gourmet foods I just must have. Unfortunately, my English Cockers are of similar opinions. They do not live for Ka-Bibble-Bits alone. They will, of course, eat ANYTHING short of tea bags ... and they'll even demolish those; but due to a complicated combination of factors comprised of me, the dogs, the nutrition experts and dog food vendors, I am drowning in a sea of conflict and problems regarding dog feeding.

First off, food is their main preoccupation in life. This has only two advantages: 1. It keeps them alive, well, and vigorous enough to steal, bark, and beg. 2. It's great for training motivation. After these two factors, it's all downhill.

Even my occasional "picky eater" is not really against food; she is only against the choice of the day, even as I may myself go on a spell of being "off" fish, or some other thing that's good for me.

At an early age, my dog savants learn all about the vast variety of edibles that regularly come in from the aforementioned two-million-acre supermarket. They have raided the grocery bags, and very often have managed to sample the packages and wrappings of some gourmet frozen entrees. So the road back to a dish of Ka-Bibble-Bits is not so eagerly taken. They will, of course, gulp down ALL their regular ration but will be all the more determined to dash into the lower shelf of the fridge when next you open it.

As to WHAT rations to feed ... well, it gets more difficult and puzzling as time goes on, with monumental advances in additives, nutrition and wonder ingredients galore. The dog food pendulum swings back and forth, from multiple additives back to plain unadulterated NO additives, all natural, just barn sweepings presumably. Dog foods (and cat foods, too) proliferate on store shelves and take up more and more space. At each visit, I see new wild brands, enticing packages, flavor names that are designed to lure the buyer and, I suspect, contents that are far from what a dog should eat. So one is wary of supermarkets. We tend to shop at shows and kennel supply shops where a similar wide selection is offered. After reading in a few dog magazines that certain renowned kennels and handlers feed all their Best in Show dogs on this or that food, you begin to have doubts as to what you're currently feeding (forgetting the 27 healthy litters you've had and the many fifteen-year-olds who have been hale and hearty to the end.) Everyone else is wondering the same. Everyone starts conferring with each other ... "What do YOU feed?" ... Phones are busy with calls on the subject, and it soon becomes apparent that the four or five new wonder foods that have nourished so many Best in Show dogs have had

From Riches to Bitches

a wide variety of effects on dogs you've heard about – some got too fat, some got too thin, many had diarrhea ... and so it goes.

All your research is for naught. So you make your own survey at a show and come home laden down with bags and bags of several varieties complete with booklets containing complicated chemical analyses, which always prove that THIS food is highly superior to all the competitors. And the competitors' foods have the same analysis claiming they're the best. Then at the bottom of the bags are blurred, fine listings of all ingredients which take a half hour and a pair of glasses to read. It's very disturbing to realize that this innocent food contains so much stuff you can't pronounce, never heard of, and have grave suspicions about. You recall those books you read telling of meat by-products being a cover-up for feet, feathers and fish heads and worse. By the time you hit the long list of totally tongue-twisting chemicals, you're really alarmed. About that time, you get a call from another breeder who has just received hot-line information from some consumers' research group that the latest preservative in almost ALL the best brands is some lethal product that was hitherto used to preserve rubber (perhaps, therefore, applicable for English

Cocker stomachs?). Anyway, you note the name of this alarming chemical containing at least 37 letters and totally unpronounceable and said to have produced three-headed puppies, ten toes, baldness and other manifestations too grisly to mention. Then back to the shows and kennel supply stores to peer at the long list of ingredients on bags only to find the dire substance in all the top brands.

Perhaps in one of the New Age Nature Food stores you find an all-organic dog food bag that boasts NO chemicals, preservatives, coloring, flavoring, salt, sugar or much else. Said to be all natural fiber and oat bran raised lovingly by some devout religious cult with primitive farm implements and no pesticides (bugs are in it as nourishing protein) and watered only with Perrier. You decide to buy a bag, fainting at the price, and your dogs, who usually eat linoleum, wallpaper and socks, hardly touch it and those that do, yuck it up. You realize you could never afford it anyway.

Then you recall the English way of dog feeding and wonder if you could manage it, the hunt for a reliable local slaughterhouse with non-steroid cattle or sheep, and how you could store mountains of tripe, hearts and other odious dog goodies. And you recall some English breeders who made their own "dog cookies" and meals and what a chore that was. You wonder if you could buy a Cusinart and do a vegetarian puree sort of thing. These ideas almost immediately appear overpowering.

For a few days, another English trick came into use ... a bowl of Mueslix cereal, veggies, and hamburger ... until someone reminded me of the red dye in the hamburger which is surely a carcinogen.

You get the picture? Where is one to turn? Meanwhile, regardless of what mess is served up, the dogs flourish and continue to gobble up all that comes their way and steal whatever doesn't.

So your own mental pendulum swings back and forth from extreme caution to a resigned "so what." You recall the very old man in the small neighborhood store buying some cans of the generic el cheapo dog food (and junk food for himself.) Out front waits old Spot, age sixteen, hale and hearty and who probably never had a balanced meal in his life.

Then I see the other side of the coin. There's a new product out ... ICE CREAM for dogs. Fido-Freeze: No sugar, no bad ingredients, made up mostly of soybeans, but good for dogs! (They say.) I can see it now: Tutti-Frutti Almond Fido-Freeze or Carob Ripple Fido-Freeze. When my English Cockers hear of this, they'll break a vein with wild excitement. I'll have to stock the freezer (the lid of which they haven't mastered). Until then, I have to take my chances on the overall daily diet, lift my eyes to St. Francis, and perhaps give 'em all half my own supper.

Perpetual Responsibility!

How many across the country are fans of Garrison Keillor and his mythical Lake Woebegone of Prairie Home Companion radio fame, I don't know, but those who are devotees of this marvelous and unique humorist will know of Father Emil's church, Our Lady of Perpetual Responsibility. If I could find this church, I'd put myself up for Chief Apostle or some such as I ,too, am a "lady of perpetual responsibility."

My cares, tasks, worries, chores, duties, ministrations, plans, plots and good deeds on behalf of my creatures are indeed perpetual. No day is long enough to encompass my rituals for the smooth and happy running of their lives at the expense of my own rest and peace.

Midnight ... ha ... more likely 2 a.m. finds me padding wearily around in old socks (mismatched, as puppies always part the pairs) doing still ONE

more thing to bring order to an already over-dogged life ... not to mention cats. All the organization plans seem to fall by the wayside and fail ... those card files, index folders, the bulletin board, the notes stuck on the fridge. One writes notes on palms with laundry markers such as "worm pill at 2 p.m." only to scrub the message off inadvertently after one of the usual clean-up jobs.

The new cat has just come home from being altered and walks about drunkenly, dazed by his misfortune which he can't yet believe; and he must be kept from knocking into Old Cat, always grumpy, who will be defended noisily by Old Dog, his lifelong love. After that is all sorted out and each person fed a sneaky snack allotted to Special Ones only, one turns, as happens a thousand times a day, to People Projects, only to recall something else on the roster of Perpetual Responsibility. Fill the bird feeders, check the automatic gallon water dispenser which always seems to be empty, then try to remember the rotation of who went out last and when, and with WHAT results, an impossible task. Remember the chicken to be boiled for broth for the puppy and the new kitten ... then don't forget to send away for the replacement parts for the Oster clipper and package up the old dull blades ... did you send off that pedigree to the lady in East Overshoe who feels her dog has mutual relatives in the family tree? And don't forget to return the cutesy puppy photos someone sent you, although you fear her address is lost.

About this time someone has to have a bone taken away as half the couch cover is knotted around it. (All couches and chairs have layers of covers!) Someone else is gnawing a hot spot on the tail. No. 2 cat has been in a fight with a mean neighborhood tom who challenged his non-existent virility, and he has come out poorly. First aid is in order; and all the dogs help, scattering the first aid kit far and wide.

Perpetual Responsibility means doing almost hourly socialization of puppies, attempting so guide their little paws on the path of right living, which is a hard road. Your Perpetual Responsibility extends to a continual awareness that absolutely NOTHING remotely edible can be put down in a vulnerable spot for a second. Not for an instant can you leave that meat loaf, cookie, candy bar, or peanut unattended. This has to be programmed into the brain, but the circuits are forever getting jammed. Every animal here loves food and will either eat, inspect, sample, nuzzle, carry off, or track through anything edible. This includes pies cooling on the porch, plates left on table edges, full trash bags with one old chicken wing in dead center. Cats are mannerly and suave about it, hopping on the dinner table with guests, sauntering about through the candles, and flicking a choice bit off a plate while humans shriek. (A line of alliteration here is not too far fetched: "The calico cat came creeping through the quiche.")

But the DOGS require more Perpetual Responsibility as there are more of them, and they can fan out and plot strategy. The kitchen disturbance over the latest theft masks the rats' nest that is being made of the guest room bed ... things like that ... then too, Perpetual Responsibility means keeping up with all sorts of complicated diets, additives, supplements, nostrums for various maladies, etc. Serving dog dinners is like a sort of combination gourmet restaurant and geriatric rest home menu where fabulous and holistic meals are served to enhance, nourish and revitalize. This process requires a wall chart and labeled stainless steel bowls, also close attention to keeping everything up to date and separate, as menus and needs tend to change. Whoever is pregnant has all sorts of weird things, A to Z, and has different ingredients than Fat One,

Growing One, Itchy One or Lean One, all of whom have a separate list of things that go in their bowls.

Good housesitters have left in despair over this chart, stating that THEIR dog gets a Gainesburger! But Perpetual Responsibility prevails even after midnight; when even your toenails are tired and at last rest seems to be at hand, you make ONE more trip down stairs to let in a forgotten cat, and ONE more trip to let out a dog ... wait ... freeze ... let her in, and almost to bed that time! But then ONE more trip down to dash off a letter for the early morning mail with the show entry you almost forgot to mail.

When you eventually put out the light and shove over the bulky snoring form of Old Dog ... THEN you recall ... AHA! ... and ONE more trip down to bring up Old Dog's pill, and to check the fire while you're down. By that time Old Dog comes down, too, and sits up arthritically for a goodie. So you have some crackers and cheese, too. It's 2 a.m. and the crated dogs get psychic and start protesting that THEY'RE left out of snack time, so each has to have a token biscuit.

Perpetual Responsibility? ... Yes, I'm the Chief Apostle without a halo, but I suspect that, like the St. Christopher that used to be on the dash of many cars until the church claimed he never existed, Our Lady of Perpetual Responsibility ranks are legion ... we're all of us!

The Convalescent

As I said before, and will say again at every opportunity, whatever dog is in need, THAT'S my favorite. And chief among the needs is convalescence. Thankfully, this doesn't happen too often, but it is bound to occur occasionally in every household. I am not a born nurse for humans, and through the years the suffering, miserable or ailing humans in my long family life have gotten somewhat less than Florence Nightingale treatment from me. Illness has always left me with psychological hangups. I never know what to do and tend to be heavy-handed, gruff and impatient. I hate to fuss with beds, fluff up pillows, manage trays, or deal with the various nasties relative to caring for someone who is laid up. For the more ambulatory person who is yet still ailing, my impatience is even more evident as I always feel their malady is somehow planned to render me a martyr and ruin my life-style.

But when the CREATURES are laid up, it is a whole different tale. I become transformed into an inexhaustible fountain of great compassion, sterling character, true dedication and tireless effort as I endeavor to return the sufferer to glowing health. I leave absolutely no stone unturned, physically or psychologically to make the hapless one a whole new being.

My hard heart melts, my crust crumbles, all my maudlin traits become apparent; I become totally overbalanced on matters of hygiene, nutrition, medication and overall care. I may be tending to a newly spayed one, or one who has just had a tumor removed. This lucky creature will have it made. During the day she will be settled in the beanbag chair with me fending off all the other animals, bringing dainty tidbits, little batches of chicken broth or some other concoction I have been laboring over a hot stove to make. I may be applying hot packs, or cold packs, or changing bandages, or giving massages. Perhaps

post-operative care!

I am entirely engrossed in hiding a pill deep within a super goodie or taking a temperature, or putting in eye drops or rubbing in salve. Whatever it is, I am hard at it around the clock, alternating with many phone calls to the vet to make sure I'm doing the right thing, or if some aberration is normal. I could be calling a fellow dog clubber for an hour about some vague new symptoms. After that, it might be time to take out the convalescent, and this excursion is conducted as though I were dealing with a baby chick. I'll tenderly conduct the patient to a special spot on the lawn for the necessaries, poking stools and observing every action in connection .

When there seems little else to do for the recovering one, I am apt to lurk about, checking the breathing, feeling an ear, opening an eyelid, and generally disturbing the patient's rest. Or maybe I hunker down by the beanbag chair and go into my most maudlin act, a long harangue of sweet talk and chatter to reassure the sickie that all is well, and that I am at the helm.

Perhaps I carry the patient up or downstairs to whatever choice bed is selected for the happy days of recovery. Wherever it is, the patient always wants somewhere else and is very apt to be restless in the night, wanting all kinds of things as all convalescents do – water or out or a different bed or the middle of mine or a goodie or just some reassurance. The dog that may have had a pill perhaps sees little green men in dreams and has to be assured they are now gone, or perhaps one must plan to stay awake all night to be sure that a patient doesn't chew off a bandage. Doze off once and it's sure to happen. Or the dog will take the time while you snooze to lick a new place raw or pull out some stitches. Best to plan for a good book and not much sleep.

Later on, when things are coming along nicely and normalcy is just around the corner, you can breathe easily, say a few prayers, and offer up a burnt offering (liver) that the nursing has paid off, and you have your dear one almost back in shape. But you still have to go easily, watch the diet, keep the walks short and not overly strenuous. In short, don't expect too much from the patient yet. However, by this time, the convalescent has developed so many spoiled rotten habits that a complete reversal to previous habits seems almost impossible. You may have to relegate your favorite, erstwhile convalescent to the low spot on the totem pole, and renew the old obedience regime.

But, there's one note of warning to all who cater to canine convalescents. Be the patient young or old, there is always SOME other soul (or more) who is totally crushed at not receiving the major share of familial attention. Should Old Dog be the center of focus, Middle Dog feels more out of it than ever. If a new mama is being pampered, the last young dog, only recently everyone's darling, keenly feels a twinge on being deposed from her pedestal. So watch it! One's duties are doubled, tripled or whatever, as all must be assured that though THEY are not sick, they're just as important as ever. A strain to be sure, but par for the convalescent course.

The Elizabethan Collar

After being in the "Dog Game" for many years, can there still be new experiences to test our souls? YES! Such a one has just been endured here at Carry-On with all its contrasting light and dark moments. There's always an old dog it seems, and the varied milestones and ravages of encroaching years must be borne for each beloved pensioner in turn. Catering to the needs of an old-timer in a multiple dog household is a self-renewing condition. Sometimes it can be handled philosophically, more often with patience sorely tried.

The latest Old Dog, a prima donna UDT, is now starring in the stellar role of medical wonder having had all her mammaries removed from one side due to a mysterious duct blockage. The excursions to the vet, tests, traumas, expenses, nursing and general upheaval can easily be imagined by any experienced dog keeper. NOW, we have a lively oldster, in fabulous spirits, star of the show, thriving on special goodies – but wearing an Elizabethan collar! This may be all very well if one has a QUIET convalescent, ailing, laid-up type of patient that dumps down in the dog bed and doesn't stir. Not so my patient.

From the first day home, she has bashed her way through every corner of a 12-room house. Amazing, but true; she has smashed into every possible piece of furniture, person, dog, cat, bush, flower, fence and tree. I suspect her collision course with everything stems from being unable to accurately gauge the width of her enormous, morning glory-shaped, plastic collar. Never deterred, she perseveres, seemingly oblivious to the impediment encasing her head, blocking out ALL peripheral vision. Also, the ungainly collar tends to drop down so that as my game convalescent dashes forward like a snowplow, vision totally obscured, she plows aside all in her path.

Tossing her a goodie is like throwing a quarter into the plastic bin at a toll booth. If she doesn't catch it, the goodie may lodge somewhere in the depths of the collar's huge bell and REMAIN THERE. Should it be a goodie with short shelf life, it must be extricated promptly or, combined with wet ear feathers ... I'm sure you get the picture.

At least nightly the contraption must be removed and sponged off, ears cleaned and dried and the whole thing reinstated for bedtime. Naturally, such a special patient must share a human bed as an Elizabethan collar is not suited to a crate! So, all night the oldster bashes about while getting comfy, all the while poking the sharp rim of her collar into the inert form of her human companion, completely depriving the latter of some much needed rest after a day of playing nurse. After a protracted session of this, the old girl decides to leave the bed. Unfortunately for nurse, it's necessary for the patient to announce her intention as the descent cannot be made unassisted with the collar intact. A downhill jump would bring rim of the collar into contact with the floor FIRST, and the patient is smart enough to realize and avoid such a potentially unpleasant episode. So, a drink from a small bowl is hand tendered, and a careful easing off the bed comes next, for the wee-hour walk when the devilish collar keeps catching a tender human leg behind the knee or on a bare portion of ankle. By the end of the Elizabethan siege, legs are battle-scarred, coffee table ornaments are long lost, screen doors dented and much else ruined. The collar itself is bent and mangled, but it has served its purpose well. On the day the vet announces it can be permanently removed, our elderly patient commemorates her freedom from the device in a private celebration. As though she had been counting off the days, she races upstairs to an obscure corner to settle down to hours of gnawing on her incision, which exercise was hitherto impossible.

A renewed spate of such chewing usually means a few MORE days with the collar on (what's left of it). It also means the other animals, people and furnishings are again subject to the ravages of the device for as long as it must be worn. Through it all my gallant pensioner, true to the tradition of unflagging British fortitude in times of hardship, carries on with all flags flying and guns blazing!

Pills and Ills

How did one ever get involved so deeply with the dogs? As the summer heat simmers on, one swats mosquitoes, worries about heartworms, fleas, the summer itch, and all else that comes with the sultry season. Those lucky enough to live at the North Pole may not have to give Caracide, and there are breeders who don't believe in putting chemicals into dogs; but those like me, who live where mosquitoes practically carry you off bodily while you sit on your porch, have to face the evil little white pills. I have been forced to find a new and better way to administer them since hot dogs, liver, and cheese have begun to fail. I find little white fragments tucked into ear feathers the next day, or into crate corners. My method is to give the "treat" when the dogs go to bed in their crates, having long ago given up trying to hide the pill in their suppers. A dog here can clean up a food dish in one minute by the inhaling method, yet leave the pill neatly on the rim, like a pearl in a stainless steel setting.

So here I come, bearing joy in a new form, but each new form palls. Hot dog sections worked for me briefly, as did liver, but both are hard to completely hide a pill in; they tend to peek through. At the first crunch, the dogs give a wounded "you-did-it-to-me-again" expression and "poing," out spurts the pill.

From Riches to Bitches

I tried a series of exotic goodies like chocolate cream pie, not a steady staple in most households; various cakes were too crumbly; and finally, a wiser dog person put me onto liverwurst! A whole new ballgame! It may not last, of course, but at the moment the pills are going down. But, at a price — I make little balls, like walnuts, with the pill in the center. So lustful are my creatures for liverwurst, and so pasty is the texture, that they wolf it down before they realize what I've done. But alas, the operation is flawed, for I, too, am a liverwurst freak! When making the walnut sized balls, I become glittery eyed and must have just ONE (larger sized) even though it's the number one no-no on my cholesterol diet list, but all reason departs at times like these...

So I grab ... and have even gotten one with a pill in it once, but it's so unique a flavor, who minds a little Caracide? After each dog has ingested his goodie, I carefully re-wrap the liverwurst and MUST have just ONE more taste (it couldn't hurt ...). I know, in my heart, however, that this small (?) lump immediately rushes to some already overburdened part of my anatomy that I have been trying vainly to reduce and also has undoubtedly deposited untold amounts of cholesterol in every vital artery. Some authorities say liverwurst puts 1000 times its weight on other bodies, and I can attest to this. A whole summer of small lumps of it for the dogs won't do THEIR figures any real good either. But then, it's sure to pall once they chance across the little white pill in the lump some day; so, then some new substance must be found. Heaven knows what, though, as there are just so many meat-based goods. We are not really a nation much given to exotic game such as octopus, woodchuck, or kangaroo. Back to the cheese shops, perhaps, where I am also forbidden by my cholesterol diet, a SUPER no-no lest my arteries require a Roto-Rooter job. But how divine is cheese of every variety, and the dogs agree! So very soon, I may be sampling little bits of Havarti, Leiderkrantz, Camembert, and the like, pondering which one is flavorful and odorous enough to camouflage the Caracide!

The end of summer will tell the end of the story: fat dogs, fat owner, heartworm, heart attacks, and other grisly things that had better not be thought about.

More Random Thoughts

WELL, IT'S COME AT LAST. People predicted it. I'm TALKING to them ... the dogs, I mean. Not just the usual, such as "good dog" or "no, no, get down," but lengthy conversations in which I supply the supposed replies. I was told long ago that people who attribute human thoughts, reactions and emotions to their pets are sick, sick, sick. At the least they are called anthropomorphists, which I cannot even spell. So here I am.

Neighbors often think I have a house full of guests due to the constant verbiage emitting from windows, doors, porch and yard. We discuss the weather on the first go-out in the morning, followed by a stream of invective against the delicate fur people (sporting dogs, too!) who answer Nature's call on the porch rather than venture onto the wet lawn.

Throughout the day various matters are discussed according to who is doing what. During a tedious grooming session, I might comment on what is coming over the FM radio, and the grooming table victim grumbles various musical opinions.

During a siesta on the couch with assorted bodies draped over me, we have a long interchange on what splendid creatures they all are, until every member is making delighted little noises of agreement.

Up in the puppy room, as each one is fussed over, toenails snipped and papers changed, there is a spirited discourse on the virtues of each one and their lovable qualities; and this is reciprocated by a chorus of delighted yips and yelps and shoelace pulling.

The fifteen-year-old, though stone deaf, is the old philosopher and the best partner for intellectual discussion when reading *Time* and commenting on the ills of the world. I think she receives my thoughts now through ESP as she pokes me with paw and nose, rumbling deep in the throat some profound canine observation. We started our conversations years ago with a few key words such as "squirrel," "bird," "supper," "car" and the like. Now we are attuned in a different way, and the younger ones pick up the key words with resultant pandemonium.

However, a good part of the dog talk is in a rougher vein, alas. For example: ME: "You rotten thing! After all I've done for you! Given you the best years of my life and spent fortunes on you! Raised you to the high echelons of education with a PhD in obedience! Mortgaged my acres on entry fees! Driven in blizzards for your post-pit shots! Bought you cases of RD Diet ... and here you are in the trash cans for the ten-zillionth time, surrounded by miles of corncobs and cantaloupe rinds, not to mention coffee grounds and old Kleenex! Is there no end to your base ingratitude? When do I ever see evidence of your sterling British breeding?" (On and on, ad nauseam.)

CRISPY, CH, and UDT: Smile-smile, wag-wag, chomp-chomp, rummage-rummage. (Exits blandly unperturbed with a tomato skin on chops as I hurl a cat food can at her portly rear.)

the Siesta

For the Geriatric

"Grow old along with me; the best is yet to be." This is a quote from the poet Robert Browning – remember him? – and Elizabeth Barrett, who had the Cocker, "Flush." Well, anyway, he lied. I'm old and can't quite envision the best yet to be, but I keep trying. It's especially hard to be ever young when the dog population seems to increase. The energy doesn't. The work does. I'm always thinking comparative thoughts, such as when I'm on my knees mopping up a puddle or worse and find I have to hang onto a nearby piece of furniture to get up. Was it just yesterday when Old Dog was having her first litter that I leapt up and down briskly during that whelping!?

Remember when Fat Dog needed some walks to reduce her girth, and I planned all that jogging? That was once – NOW I can hardly waddle along with any of them as they pull me along like a sled-dog team.

It takes twice as long nowadays to feed the horde, and leaning down to place the feed pans is hazardous as I'm not as agile as I was and get smashed in the nose as the eager ones leap up. Then all the pans have to be picked up, and we go through it all again, and I end up puffing .

The trainers all tell you to have a training session heeling the dog briskly while you keep up a non-stop cheery talk in a high and happy voice, saying, "That's it! Good dog! Watch me!" and the like. I find that walking briskly is ENOUGH without the chatter, so I'm out of breath again.

I used to like to lie down on the couch for a brief siesta with a dog or two just to have a nap; but now if I do that, I'm apt to completely conk out and not wake for hours and never notice that they are chewing the couch arms off!

I find I'm not as quick to rescue my own sandwich from leaping jaws as I used to be. I find that a long grooming session leaves me worn out and that the dogs are far heavier nowadays when hauled up on the table. Leaning over the bath tub with a soaked dog isn't the fun it used to be. And I find I'm getting too fat to crawl into the crates to rescue balls and toys and get out the mattresses for the laundry. I'm apt to let a lot of things slip that I would never have before, and I'm making excuses for myself.

Run to your library and get a copy of *Discover* magazine for October, 1994. It's a rather far-out scientific publication with articles I can barely grasp, but there's a great one on dogs with lots of photos and even a great skeleton. It tells the latest findings on how dogs split off from wolves and perhaps got the short end of the stick genetically. What caught my eye was the statement that most, if not all, dogs are stuck in adolescence! Right on! I've got a houseful of them – difficult teenagers right up to age 15! And with all this, I'm going down the sunset slope myself!

Every time I take one of my many geriatric pills, some dog comes out of nowhere and tries to grab it thinking it's a goodie. I don't move as lightning fast as I used to, so I can't avoid the Old Dog bumbling underfoot; I always fall against some hard piece of furniture, getting black and blue. As for the swift running youngsters, it's hopeless to leap out of their way with my stiff knee, so here comes another fall ... maybe the padding on the old body is a blessing!

And I'm not as swift in the upper story as I was. Someone calls up to tell a long, happy story about little Snuffy they bought a year ago; and, for the life of me, I can't recall who the sire and dam were. This is not to mention the one who calls who got her dog TEN years ago and he's going strong – which is more than I can say for me!

Old friends mean well when they tell me that it's best to just cut down, have fewer dogs, give up tracking before I fall in a woodchuck hole, take it easy, etc., etc. But somehow that seems to be throwing in the towel.

I plan to keep going, keep pitching, keep slogging along as I have my eye on a GREAT breeding for that orange bitch and a UDT for the talented one, not to mention a few youngsters who need CDs. What has to be eased off is the HOUSEWORK ... par for the course!

Tribute to an Old Timer

Time marches on, and beloved "Old Dog" may not be with me much longer. At fifteen, a victim of two strokes and a possible brain tumor, she is just wearing out. There is nothing like an old and infirm dog to try one's nerves, but all through it is the thread of heartbreak and self recrimination when I am irked at some episode only to realize that it may soon be all over.

Old Dog dodders about and is constantly falling over. She is deaf and thus cannot respond; so all calling is done by poking her to get her attention, or going after her as she meanders aimlessly about the yard. I marvel at the wonderful fortitude and patient courage with which she so uncomplainingly accepts her great limitations. Philosophical and wise, she has come to terms with pain, discomfort and frustrations. Her devotion remains unchanged however.

She is hard to feed, hard to give pills to, uncertain as to plumbing, and somewhat unsightly with warts and a hint of BO. But oh, the glorious memories of her when she arrived as a pup, the wildest thing alive, and of her early years amassing trophies in the obedience ring, and when she attained the very first UDT of her breed. No dog ever had a larger vocabulary, and she would even alert for "squash" because it sounded like the start of "squirrel."

The youngest one is now enamored of Old Dog and has a passionate love affair with the old lady, often bowling her off her feet and dancing upon her amiable inert form, kissing and washing the old face, and trying to express the enormity of her puppy love for the matriarch of the household.

After pill time, all the dogs gather around to await Old Dog's bedtime Gainesburger and to greedily pick fragments from her feathers as she isn't too swift at table manners anymore and consequently dribbles food everywhere. Everyone in the canine crew respects Old Dog somehow, and seems to give her a chance to get out the door, or to avoid knocking her over in the rush.

Memories come flooding back of another Old Dog some fifteen years ago, who wore out in much the same way, yet lingered on past the day when I should have "done the deed." Somehow the generations of others who have come between have not erased the images that come to mind of Old Dogs through the years, with patient eyes, unsure steps and that devotion that goes to the very end, following you about at every move, afraid that somehow the last hour will come and they might not be with you. Much time is spent in sleep, with twitching paws and soft snores. I wonder what glories of the past might be running through the old head ... better days, lost puppyhood.

When Old Dog goes, there will be a pall on the house for some time, trial though she may have been at the end. None of the young hopefuls seem to have the depth somehow, nor the soul which comes only with old age and the peculiar patience and philosophy that only a fine old dog can attain. The youngest will miss her, never knowing that some day she, too, will be Old Dog and will again wrench my heart.

Thieves of Time

W hen I was in junior high school a million years ago, I wrote for the school magazine. Recently, while in the attic putting out totally useless mothballs to repel squirrels (as well as high-frequency devices that repel me, not them ...) I ran across a copy of the long ago magazine. Once I got over the shock of the date and realizing I was still alive enough to climb the attic stairs, I read again my 1935 masterpiece entitled "Thieves of Time." Based on the facts of the day, it revealed the roots of my present life. All I had was one neurotic cat and a white rat. But a lot of time was stolen away tending and interacting with these dependents.

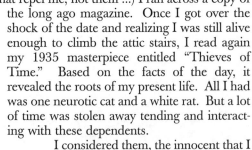

I considered them, the innocent that I was ... as Thieves of Time. I couldn't pass them without communing, feeding, petting or cleaning up after them. The seeds were sown!

Things never went anywhere but down after that.

I wasn't allowed a dog during those early Boston years, but I plotted and schemed. I hung around with and collected neighborhood mongrels like a Canine Pied Piper. (See what can happen to a child who is deprived of canine companionship!) When the Great Day finally came and I was through with my educational adventures, I took the plunge and got my first spaniel, and then soon another ... and a litter ... and on and on! And if I ever thought a lone cat and a white rat took up time, I didn't know what lay ahead.

Talk about Thieves of Time – well, time and schedules and leisure flew out the window as I plunged into the dog clubs, training, tracking, grooming, drill teams, shows, etc. But it was still under SOME sort of control, and I had enough time ... barely ... as yet unstolen to follow a career.

But like all absorbing avocations, it encroached like creeping happy fungus. The more I became immersed in dogs, the more I had to learn, study and do. More time and more time was always set aside for the furry ones, as they proliferated steadily.

The years have passed, like a flash it would seem, and here I am in the attic, dead spiders in my hair, reading about "Thieves of Time" while several of the younger dogs fight to climb the steep attic stairs. Nowadays my time has ALL been stolen away. I have to try to steal some back for non-doggy things like eating and sleeping. I'm not just talking about the usual needs of a horde of dogs that eat up my time, as we all know about the feeding, mopping, disinfecting, exercising, training, finding new ways to disguise pills, and all that. I'm suddenly becoming aware of OTHER thieves of time that are now adding up to more hours than I'm allotted every day. How many times have I painfully restuffed and sewed up poor Raccoon, the favorite plush toy who never seems to last long? Will I ever stop cleaning off tennis balls someone has carried to the dog yard and dropped in a doo-doo? Can I ever hope to pass the towering piles of old *Gazettes*, *Dog Worlds*, *Quarterlies*, and *Dog News* without flicking out "just one" to browse through; a long session grows longer as I usually search back in other piles for previous articles.

Who tots up the hours hunting for the one missing sock, glove or undergarment? Who would be so coldly calculating as to consider time lost when one succumbs to a sojourn on the den couch with several mushers ... or the hours spent cheering up the under-the-weather one who has just been spayed? Not to mention the pregnant one who is so uncomfortable and must have you near her all the time. And what about those many hours when work seems to stop because you're grieving and desolate after putting an old one to sleep because it's time, though the time is never right ... And when those little ones come who are at first just mindless lumps, all your time will be spent just beaming at them, watching them shift and twitch, and worrying if you're doing all you should for them.

If an incautious stumble should knock over one of those MANY shoe boxes of photos going back years that you never had time to paste into albums, then more masses of time will fly away. So many candids you foolishly didn't date or label ... WHOSE puppies are those? When? Where did THAT one go? HE was certainly championship material! This may well lead to getting out your tangled masses of pedigrees which really OUGHT to be all computerized, but you never got to it. That lengthy study sparks a new time-con-

From Riches to Bitches

suming interest, and you rush to the typewriter to write to a few people to ask about puppies, now grown up ... and talk genetics.

Much of this involvement may lead to a temporary lack of observation as to what the dozen or so "home raised" dogs are up to. It's usually bad news. They know when you're absorbed in other pursuits and take advantage to quietly rearrange something, such as the couch, the slipcovers, broom and mop, a left shoe, your best African violets, or the kitty litterbox (a favorite). The amount of time you spent doing interesting doggy-related research equates about equally with the clean-up and repair you'll do later. Then, feeling guilty, you spend some "personal time" with the dogs, throwing balls, playing games, taking walks, and teaching them new tricks with goodies. There's really very little escape if you've traveled the Doggy Path into this deep rut of dedication.

Perhaps ONE evening you set aside for some totally non-doggy pursuit ... and the phone rings. It is a breeder you've never met who has heard you had some experience with a new malady and would like to chat an hour or two about vets, pills, diets, etc., ending up with a jolly account of all the cute things her dogs are doing! Perhaps you were caught cleaning the china cabinet. The Windex has long ago dried on your fingers, and you've forgotten the project since it's such fun talking. You know you'll never get at the china cabinet anyway. The last cleaning lady quit, saying that the trophies, ribbons, and figurines were too much for her, not to mention the dog dust-bunnies.

So ... in 1935, with one cat and a white rat, I never envisioned all this. But perhaps it was deep in my subconscious all the time, and I'm just working out my own destiny.